The McKenna Legacy...
A Legacy of Love

To my darling grandchildren,

I leave you my love and more. Within thirty-three days of your thirty-third birthday — enough time to know what you are about — you will have in your grasp a legacy of which your dreams are made. Dreams are not always tangible things, but more often are born in the heart. Act selflessly in another's behalf, and my legacy will be yours.

Your loving grandmother,
Moira McKenna

P.S. Use any other inheritance from me wisely and only for good, lest you destroy yourself or those you love.

Dear Reader,

The idea for THE McKENNA LEGACY came to me upon receipt of a family tree, painstakingly researched by a member of my family—not a McKenna, but an uncle who married into the clan. I'd always been fascinated by my Irish ancestors and yet knew very little about them (other than my aunts, uncles and first cousins), since they settled in New York, while I've always lived in Chicago. A "first cousin once removed," who also had worked up a family tree, gave me firsthand insight into my grandmother Rose's seven McKenna siblings.

While *See Me in Your Dreams, Tell Me No Lies* and *Touch Me in the Dark* don't recount real adventures, I wrote them with love and with my own extended family in mind. Perhaps my relatives will recognize certain glimmers of truth about themselves in some of the characters— especially about the caring I have always felt when among them.

I hope you'll love the McKennas, too, and will look forward to hearing from more of them in the future.

Patricia Rosemoor

See Me in Your Dreams
Patricia Rosemoor

Harlequin Books

TORONTO • NEW YORK • LONDON
AMSTERDAM • PARIS • SYDNEY • HAMBURG
STOCKHOLM • ATHENS • TOKYO • MILAN
MADRID • WARSAW • BUDAPEST • AUCKLAND

To all of the McKennas, living and deceased, who are or have been part of my extended family.

Special thanks to those who took it upon themselves to chronicle the McKenna clan. My uncle, George Willett, a McKenna by marriage, inspired the idea for The McKenna Legacy. And my first cousin once removed, Gerardine Masino, shared with me her memories of relatives distanced only by the miles between Chicago and New York.

ISBN 0-373-22382-X

SEE ME IN YOUR DREAMS

Copyright © 1996 by Patricia Pinianski

This edition published by arrangement with Harlequin Books S.A.

® and TM are trademarks of the publisher. Trademarks indicated with ® are registered in the United States Patent and Trademark Office, the Canadian Trade Marks Office and in other countries.

Printed in U.S.A.

McKENNA FAMILY TREE

Descendants of MOIRA KELLY McKENNA

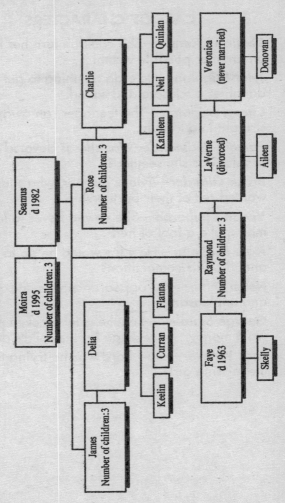

CAST OF CHARACTERS

Keelin McKenna—She couldn't turn her back on another possible victim.

Tyler Leighton—He'd do anything to get his daughter back safe and sound.

Cheryl Leighton—The teenager ran away... straight into trouble.

Pamela Redmond—Was she as devoted an assistant as she seemed?

Brock Olander—Tyler's partner, who suddenly wanted out of their partnership.

Vivian Claiborne—She vowed never to let any man make a fool of her.

Nate Feldman—How far would he go to get ahead of his competition?

Helen Dunn—Her appearance was unexpected and unpleasant.

George Smialek—Did the grief-stricken parent want money...or revenge for his child's death?

Jack Weaver—How hard was he trying to find the missing girl?

Prologue

The dark swallowed her whole, making her feel smaller than ever. She lay frozen. Waiting. Counting the seconds . . . the minutes . . . the hours.

Finally, the house grew perfectly still.

Her ragged breath piercing the silence, she gathered her courage and slipped out of bed. She threw off her nightshirt, tugged on soft jeans and an even softer T-shirt. The familiar cotton garments soothed her flesh, which was pebbling despite the warmth of the June night.

She acknowledged her fear, and as she stuffed a change of clothing, a sweater and a few personal items into a backpack, her thoughts were as liquid as the waves washing onto shore outside her window.

Can't stay here any longer. Not one minute. No more lies.

She buckled up the backpack. Her hands shook, making her bracelet resonate. Strands of leather intertwined with ancient charms and symbols that she didn't fully understand—and that had somehow become a part of her—tinkled like a fairy wind chime.

Scooting her stockinged feet into her high-tops, she took a deep breath. She was ready. Except for money.

She didn't have enough. She knew where some cash was, though. She'd have to take it.

That would make me a thief, *she thought uneasily.*

No worse than a liar, *an inner voice countered.*

A thrill shooting down her spine, she sneaked down the stairs, avoiding the one that creaked. A moment later, she was in his study, ransacking his desk for the handful of tens and twenties he always kept in case of an emergency. She stuffed the cash into her wallet, then the wallet into her jeans pocket.

Returning to the foot of the stairs, the backpack's straps secured around her shoulders, she stopped for a moment, tears gathering in her eyes...a lump in her throat threatening to choke her.

Why did he do it? Why? Now that I know, everything is ruined.

Sick inside, she rushed toward the front door, knocking into the pedestal, making the new stone sculpture teeter on its base. She caught and steadied the free form that reminded her of an angel about to take flight. Her pulse drumming so loudly it could be heard in the farthest reaches of the house, she fled the dwelling as if the hounds of hell were on her heels. She burst into the moonless night, unseeing, moving by rote, tracing her way down into the ravine.

Brush thrashed around her legs. Gasps broke from her heaving chest. Lake water battered the nearby shoreline.

Nothing could drown out the frightened beat of her heart.

Chapter One

County Cork, Éire

As always, when Keelin McKenna entered the work shed behind the old-fashioned thatch-roofed cottage, she sorely missed the solid if diminutive presence who had been part of the place for so many decades. She passed under the bunches of drying herbs and other plants hanging from the rafters, inhaling deeply as she approached the workbench. The healing scents helped assuage her sorrow, which was becoming more distant with each passing day. Not that she would ever forget Moira McKenna.

The year before, at ninety-three, the elderly woman had finally relinquished her earthly existence to join her late, much beloved husband, Seamus, and had left Keelin her most precious possession—the bit of land with its cottage amid a field of wild herbs and a carefully cultivated supplemental garden. Over the decades, some of the locals had appointed Moira McKenna healer, while others had disparaged her as a witch. Keelin had called the dear woman Gran.

Knowledge of potions and poultices gathered over the years, from the time she was a toddler at her grandmother's knee, added to the spirit that made her want to help others—these were Keelin's true inheritance from the woman who had been the backbone of the McKenna clan.

She didn't want to think about the other...the darkness that dwelled deep inside her. That, too, had been one of Moira's many facets...that had made them both different.

She shook away the traces of last night's frightening dream and concentrated instead on her purpose. If only her stubborn father had listened to her—if only her voice had been stronger, Keelin thought guiltily—perhaps Da would not have had the heart attack that almost killed him. Well, if she hadn't been vigilant enough before, she would do what she could now.

Wanting to be at the main house when her father arrived home from hospital, she hurriedly gathered the supplies she needed—root of valerian and dried blue lavender blossoms. Mixing them together, she placed a small handful in each of a dozen muslin pouches. When suspended beneath the tap so that hot water flowed through them, the herbs would make an exquisitely scented fresh infusion that would also be soothing, hopefully relaxing her quick-tempered father and helping him to attain the restful sleep so necessary to healing.

Undoubtedly he would refuse any more-advanced remedies from her. But even if he scorned it, rolled his eyes and shook his head as he was wont to do over things he didn't understand, this she could do for him. And one other thing. A truly momentous thing. Perhaps she could bring him some inner peace.

But how to make her announcement?

After tying off the last pouch, Keelin gathered all of them together in a basket, left the shed and headed across the field of wild herbs and over the rolling pasture toward her parents' home. And just in time. Her brother, Curran, and sister, Flanna, were helping Da from the car, while Ma and Great-aunt Marcella, on short leave from the convent that had been her home for her entire adult life, looked on.

Basket swinging from her arm, thick auburn hair whipping around her face, Keelin ran to join them. "Da!" she yelled.

James McKenna turned to wave at his oldest daughter. His white hair reflected only glimpses of the red that had once crowned his head. His eyes, though, were still as green as the surrounding fields, where cows with new calves grazed. They were Moira's eyes. And Flanna's eyes. Like Curran, Keelin had inherited their mother's gray.

Keelin enveloped the wiry body that should have withstood the curse of high cholesterol, even if her father was a dairy farmer. "How are you doing, Da?"

"Just grand. Good as new."

But she could see the lie to Da's words in his eyes. He might be recovering physically, but his near-death experience had affected him deep in his soul, whether or not he would admit it. The reason she had to act, to set things right in the family.

"See, the sun has even made an appearance to greet me," he said expansively, raising his face to the golden rays.

Auspicious, Keelin thought, for the weather was more fickle than any lover. Most days were soft with the mist that greened the fields year-round. But the sun could pop in and out in the blink of an eye. On any excursion, she could take an umbrella and a swimsuit, for she was sure to have the opportunity to use both.

"Get yourself in the house, James Joseph McKenna, before you expire from heat exhaustion," her mother, Delia, demanded. A handsome woman, her skin smooth and only a bit of silver threading her black hair, she appeared far younger than Da, though only five years separated them. "Come along now."

Her father shook his head and made a sound of exasperation even while following her orders. "No need to fuss, woman."

Knowing he loved being fussed over, Keelin exchanged grins with Curran and Flanna. They linked arms, taking up the rear of the group, as they entered the two-story limestone house that had for many years sheltered Keelin's grandparents, her parents and her younger siblings. After Seamus died, however, her grandmother had moved back to her old cottage. Then, lured away by fine horseflesh, Curran had gone off to Galway; Flanna had entered university in Dublin, after which she'd chosen to stay in the city to design her jewelry; while Keelin herself had taken a flat in Cork to be near the herbalist shop she ran with two other women. That is, until Moira's inheritance had made her a commuter.

At the doorway, Keelin automatically dipped her fingers into the small font of holy water and crossed herself as she entered the foyer. For the past several years, only her parents had wandered the rambling rooms with tall bay windows and views of the year-round green, rolling pastures. Except for holidays and the like, when grand stories and laughter once more filled the house. Perhaps she would be able to make certain that soon more such occasions would present themselves, Keelin thought with hope, still wondering how she would tell Da what she was about to do.

Her father settled in his great stuffed chair before the stone fireplace and looked around. "Ah, this is satisfying to a simple man such as myself. Having me whole family in attendance."

"Not your *whole* family," Marcella corrected him, straightening the collar of her habit. The elderly nun had never been one to mince words.

"Now, Sister Mary, don't you be bringing *them* up," he complained.

"Da, it was *you* who brought up the subject when you were in a desperate way," Flanna reminded him. "You wished the three of you could be together one last time before you died!"

Bless her soul, Keelin thought, gathering her courage.

"Well, I didn't die, did I? And they didn't care enough to come to my side when I was near death, so why should I be giving them a thought?" he said with the full drama of a true Irishman sorely beleaguered.

"Ah, Da, you're being unreasonable," Curran said, swiping his thick black hair away from his forehead. "You wouldn't let us contact them so they would know you were sick in the first place."

"You always did have a bit o' the blarney in you, James. Tsk, tsk, tsk," Delia teased, true to her Murphy upbringing. "You know you want a wee peek at Rose and Raymond again...." She suddenly sobered. "God willing."

An uneasy silence settled around them. Keelin hadn't considered her aunt or uncle might have gone on—and her never having set eyes on either of them.

She couldn't tell Himself what she was about, then. Couldn't raise Da's hopes. A refusal from one of the other two triplets would be bad enough. But if one of them weren't even alive . . .

Shaking away the chilling thought, Keelin quickly recovered. "I have an announcement." Though not the one she'd intended.

Five pairs of quizzical eyes turned to her.

"What is it, lass?" Da asked.

"I'm going on a trip. Tomorrow morning, as a matter of fact. Business." Her mouth went dry with the lie. "To meet with other herbalists." Heat rose along her neck like fairy fire. "And it's out of the country."

"Where to?"

Taking a deep breath, she said, "America," and waited for an explosion of temper.

"DA'S SUSPICIOUS, you know."

The expected outburst never having come from her father, Keelin still pretended innocence as she and Flanna entered her whitewashed, thatch-roofed cottage after supper. "Of what?"

"I'm neither blind nor daft, Keelin. Nor is anyone else in our family. Everyone is feigning ignorance, when in truth your intentions to contact Aunt Rose and Uncle Raymond are as clear as the waters of Lough Danaan," she said, referring to the small lake edging the McKenna property.

Keelin moved to the peat-burning stove, where the kettle was on the boil. "You do know me."

"You never could tell a falsehood without turning as red as your hair."

So true. Keelin sighed. "Tea?"

"That'd be grand."

The cottage was merely two rooms, the larger for living, the smaller for sleeping—part of the original bedroom having been converted to a bath. Keelin loved Moira's old house, the place where her grandmother had lived alone before Seamus had come to her rescue when she was in dire straits, and she in turn had tamed his wild heart. The cottage was simple, as were the furnishings, but neither mattered to Keelin.

While she prepared the relaxing chamomile, Flanna fetched the mugs and placed them on the table, then searched the icebox for a lemon and milk. No words passed between them. They'd always had a special rapport, working together seamlessly, as if they had somehow been connected in the womb despite the three years between them. Connected and yet nothing alike. Green eyed, strawberry blonde, petite but well filled out, Flanna turned heads. And she was as bold as they came, unlike Keelin, who sometimes envied her younger sister's outgoing spirit and sense of adventure. By comparison, she was a mouse.

"So how will you go about it?" Flanna asked when Keelin set down the teapot and slid into a vacant chair.

Keelin poured the steaming, aromatic liquid. "Several of the American cousins wrote Gran. She kept the letters in their envelopes, so I have the addresses."

"Then you'll approach Raymond and Rose through their children." Flanna squeezed a slice of lemon in her tea.

Adding a bit of milk to hers, Keelin nodded. "I thought it a wise idea. I'm certain I'll be needing their help in reuniting three of the most stubborn Irish I've ever heard tell of."

"The wound goes deep—more than thirty years."

"Long enough."

"Aye."

Dreamily, Keelin sipped at her tea. "I was imagining how grand it would be if they could celebrate their sixtieth birthday together this October with as many McKennas as could be gathered round them."

"If Rose and Raymond are both still alive," Flanna said softly, echoing Keelin's worst fear.

"They must be. For Da's sake."

Later, after Flanna left to retire to the bedroom their parents kept for her, Keelin had reason to further contemplate birthdays. She'd passed her thirty-third unnoticed while Da was in hospital. The day had transpired like any other...except for her thinking heavily on Moira's last words to her.

Entering the bedroom, she lifted the top of the ancient music box that she'd bought from a Traveler recently, and removed a thick, cream-colored sheet of paper. She sat on the edge of her lace-trimmed bed to study once again the missive written in her grandmother's steady hand.

To my darling Keelin,

I leave you my love and more. Within thirty-three days after your thirty-third birthday—enough time to know what you are about—you will have in your grasp a legacy of which your dreams are made. Dreams are not always tangible things, but more often are born in the heart. Act selflessly in another's behalf, and my legacy shall be yours.

Your loving grandmother,
Moira McKenna

P.S. Use any other inheritance from me wisely and only for good lest you harm yourself or those you love.

Flanna and Curran both had received similar missives, and Keelin supposed the thick cream envelopes the solicitor had sent to the American cousins held the same message. She had been well and truly caught by the spirit of Moira's bequest to her grandchildren. Moira had wanted them to be happy, especially since her own children had tainted their personal lives with intolerance and jealousy.

Keelin and her siblings had pored over the letter together several times throughout the past year, wondering if their grandmother, truly something of a *bean feasa*—an old woman with magical powers—could have seen into their futures. They'd wondered if there was any validity to this legacy that fascinated yet burdened each inheritor.

Keelin read Gran's words again: "Within thirty-three days after your thirty-third birthday..."

Only a few weeks to go.

And the reference to dreams reminded her of the one she'd had the night before.

Act selflessly in another's behalf...

Keelin swept away a nagging guilt. This dream was different from the last time, she assured herself. Different from all the others. She didn't know the eyes she saw through. They belonged to a stranger in a strange place. Therefore, she had no control.

Perhaps it had been just a dream, she thought desperately, rather than one of her dreaded night terrors. Keelin pondered the dream. A young girl running away—and her off to America. Of course. That's all it was.

Had to be.

THE CITY WAS ALWAYS a scary place. At night, it was even worse, overflowing with menacing people. Raggedy homeless with blank stares. Uniformed policemen with too-sharp gazes. Billed-capped gang members with hot, hungry eyes.

The stuff of nightmares.

She wasn't very brave, but she forced herself to continue on. Hands stuffed into pockets, head down so she wouldn't have to look at anyone, she rushed east along Monroe Street, taking the bridge over the railroad yard. One foot in front of the other.

Left. Right. Left. Right.

Music beckoned her like a pied piper.

Almost there. Almost there.

She hurried across the edge of the lawn, dodging a hand-holding couple. Skirting a bag woman leaning against her shopping cart of belongings. Losing herself at the back of a crowd of middle-aged people with their fancy fold-up chairs, lit candles and glasses of fine wine.

In the distance stood Navy Pier with its giant Ferris wheel a lit beacon. She turned. Band shell and illuminated city skyline before her, she slumped to the grass, winded.

Afraid. Always afraid.

Tears flooded her eyes, but she slashed them away. She'd had no choice. She had to make the best of it.

How long?

She tried concentrating on the music, but it was classical stuff like he played. Liszt, she thought. Why that? Anything else would have been better. Anything not a reminder...

She closed her eyes, covered her mouth and rocked. She could see him—dark hair swept across his brow, pale blue eyes sparkling as he laughed with her, hugged her tight.

Lies. All lies.

The enormity of what she'd done hit her suddenly, and she began to shake inside. It took all her will-power not to scream, not to get up in front of all these people and beg for help. They would only make her go back.

Blindly, she reached for her bracelet. Her fingers twined through the leather strands. Traced one charm, then another. Their familiar touch calmed her. With great effort, she settled down. Took deep breaths. Told herself everything was going to be all right.

Then the voice behind her saying, "There you are!" made her jerk, causing the charms to tinkle and her to whirl around so fast that something flew from her fingers and her head spun....

HEAD SPINNING, Keelin sat straight up in her seat, her body covered in a light sweat. For a moment, she was dazed, disoriented. Until Liszt faded into the drone of jet engines, and she realized she was on the plane to Chicago.

Another dream. The same eyes. The same fear. Fear that she could taste as if it were her own.

She trembled inside at haunting memories... at old guilt... at her inability to act when it counted. Now it was happening again... but this time she didn't know who it was.

Dear God, no. Not again.

Surely she couldn't be held responsible for yet another life.

Chicago

"I'M IMPRESSED. You really came all the way from Ireland for the sole purpose of talking my father and Aunt Rose into visiting the old sod for a reunion?"

Keelin stared across a slick black-lacquered desk scattered with folders and videotapes. Her cousin Skelly McKenna, her uncle Raymond's oldest child, leaned back in his chair, his hands behind his head. She searched his expression for any trace of mockery, but he seemed genuinely impressed.

"Da almost died, and on his sickbed admitted he wished to see his brother and sister again. I'm certain if the situations were reversed, you would do the same for *your* father."

Skelly laughed, the sound tinged with bitterness. "My father would never say such a thing to me. We're not exactly what you would call close."

Not exactly what Keelin wanted to hear. "Are you telling me you won't help?"

"Not at all. But I am telling you that *I* don't have a lot of influence with Dad." Skelly rose and paced the spacious office, outfitted with more black-lacquered furniture and a couple of overstuffed black love seats. The only color in the room came from the Oriental carpet and a few well-placed pieces of artwork on the walls. "My sister Aileen, on the other hand, continues to charm the socks off the old man, and I'm sure we can enlist her aid when Dad gets back from Washington."

Raymond McKenna was a U.S. congressman from Chicago.

Relief swept through Keelin. "I dreaded doing this alone."

"Hey, cuz, I'll do whatever I can for the cause," Skelly said with a wicked smile that dimpled one cheek.

Keelin started. "Grandad."

"What?"

"Your smile...you reminded me of him just then." With his black hair, blue eyes, that smile, dimple and all...Skelly looked exactly like a young Seamus McKenna.

"That's right. You knew old Seamus."

"That I did."

"You knew Moira pretty well, too, right?" Skelly asked, settling his hip on the edge of his desk.

"Of course."

"Was she...*okay* just before she died? I mean here." He tapped his forehead.

Putting Keelin on edge. The spacious office suddenly seemed to close in on her. "Gran was the wisest woman I ever had the privilege to know," she informed him stiffly. "And that, until the day she died."

"Well, *after* she died, I got this strange letter...."

"Ah, the legacy." She relaxed.

"You know about it, then?"

"I received the letter, as well, as did my brother and sister. I believe she wrote what was in her heart for each of her nine grandchildren because her own children had acted so unwisely."

"Nicely put," he said, a cynical note in his tone.

And why shouldn't he be a bit cynical? Keelin thought. An anchor for "The Whole Story," a tab-

loid news show, Skelly reported stories that often laid
open people's terrible secrets for all to dissect. Though
she didn't care for tabloid journalism herself, neither
televised nor print, she was not about to judge this
cousin whom she'd just met. Who knew what road
had brought him to his place in life?

"You'll have to tell me more about Moira later,"
Skelly said, rising. "But at the moment, I need to get
to makeup. I'm taping this afternoon's show in forty-
five minutes."

"Well, then." She stood. "I'm at the Hotel Clareton—"

"Hey, I'm not chasing you out. Stay and watch the
telecast. We'll do lunch."

Do lunch? Realizing Skelly meant they should eat
together, she thought Americans certainly had some
unusual expressions.

"You're certain I wouldn't be in the way?"

"You're too polite to get in anyone's way."

So, a short while later, Keelin sat in a back corner of
the busy control room. Having lived a simple life
mostly close to the land, she was a bit intimidated by
all the technology and the fast pace that was part of
Skelly's world. Looking through the plate-glass window to the studio, she could see technicians adjusting
lighting and sound equipment. In the control room,
others talked over headphones, while images flashed
across the monitors, some at double speed.

One particular image caught her interest. A man's
face filled the screen. His features were handsome,
strong, magnetic, his expression intense. From the pale
eyes looking out at her as he spoke—the sound was
down, so she couldn't hear his words—she sensed both
strength and heartbreaking emotion. She couldn't tear

her gaze from the monitor, and so when the next image flashed across the small screen, she felt as if she were suddenly sucked inside.

A young girl, barely a teenager, her light brown hair flying around her pretty face...

Something about the girl...Keelin felt a strong connection.

Then the monitor went blank, and Keelin sat staring, her heart pounding loud enough to drown out the raucous voices in the booth.

She didn't know how long she sat there in stunned silence, mind spinning. It couldn't be. She was in denial as the show began. Teasers introduced the day's stories, but the words didn't mean anything to Keelin until the girl's image multiplied on several monitors.

"...and then we have a story we see every day," Skelly intoned in an authoritative voice. "Teenagers vanishing from their homes. But did Cheryl Leighton run away, as the police report indicates, or was she the victim of foul play, as her father, real-estate magnate Tyler Leighton, wants us to believe?"

Sitting through the first two stories and the myriad commercials of the half-hour program was the most difficult twenty minutes Keelin ever spent. She kept telling herself she was mistaken. There could be no connection. She'd imagined it.

But Cheryl Leighton had disappeared...and her dream had been of a runaway, the setting some unknown American city.

On edge, she watched footage of the girl and her father at some kind of building-christening ceremony, as Skelly explained, "Two nights ago, fourteen-year-old Cheryl Leighton disappeared from the North Bluff home she shares with her widowed father. So far in the investigation, the police have turned up no evidence of foul play.''

Then, before that same home—a mansion on a bluff overlooking the lake—her father spoke to the camera. "Cheryl wouldn't have run away," Tyler Leighton insisted. "She had no reason. She was a happy kid. A normal kid. She wasn't involved in gangs or drugs. We had a great relationship. We never even fought.''

But a flash of something unsettling in his pale blue eyes put a lie to those words, Keelin thought. Something he wasn't saying.

Why did he do it? Why? Now that I know, everything is ruined.

Fragments of the dreams whirled through Keelin's head. She replayed them to the best of her ability. In her mind, the girl was fiddling with her bracelet, taking succor from the familiar sound of the tinkling charms, when Keelin caught sight of the very same bracelet on the monitor. Her eyes widened as the proof transfixed her.

Then *his* image returned to the screen. The father. The *reason* the girl had run.

"All I want is my daughter back," he was saying grimly. "Home and safe. I'll do *anything* to make that happen."

And Keelin realized she would do anything, as well. This couldn't turn out like the last time. Dear God, she would never be able to live with herself if something desperate happened to Cheryl Leighton.

But how to go about finding her?

Putting her trust in a cousin who had no idea of what he was dealing with, she cornered Skelly directly after the taping and insisted they return to the privacy of his office, where they could talk without being overheard.

The moment the door was closed behind them, she said, "I know you'll find this hard to believe, but I have a connection to the Leighton girl."

"What kind of a connection?"

"The kind I sometimes get through a dream."

"A dream," he echoed, settling his hip on the edge of his desk.

She'd seen that look before. Mocking disbelief. Not that she could blame him. Pacing to assuage her nerves, she told Skelly only the minimum. Not the details of her worst night terrors. She focused on the current situation, briefly encapsulating both incidents.

"In the past, the dreams have always been connected to someone I knew or at least had met," Keelin then told him. "This was different. I thought maybe it was just a simple dream because I had no idea who the girl was. Or *where* she was, for that matter. Now I know the big American-looking city in the second dream obviously is Chicago, because Cheryl Leighton is the girl." She indicated her wrist. "That unusual bracelet she was wearing in the news footage...I saw it twice before."

Unable to discern whether Skelly believed her, she tensely waited for his reaction. That he said "You know this sounds absurd" didn't thrill her.

"The dreams are not something I asked for or want, Skelly...no more than Gran did. It's part of her inheritance...at least for me."

He scowled. "Dad did say something about his mother being considered a bit fey."

"You don't have to believe, Skelly. Just help me. Help Cheryl Leighton."

"If you really know something that'll help find her, you should go to the police."

"No authorities." Once was enough. She shuddered, remembering the consequences. "I've had a bad experience with that," was all she would say, though.

"What, then?"

"First, help me get to Tyler Leighton."

Skelly was thoughtful. "That's doable. He runs L&O Realty." Then his expression grew shrewd. "I tell you what. I'll make you a deal. I help you get whatever information you need...then you help me. We find the Leighton girl, and I get the exclusive. We can do a whole program on this case and your abilities—"

"No!"

"No?"

"Absolutely not!" Keelin could hardly believe what he was suggesting. "I won't be paraded before your countrymen like some kind of freak."

"Not a freak. A sensation. Talk-show hosts will be clamoring for you—"

"No," Keelin repeated, more calmly this time. "I won't let you exploit something that even I don't fully understand." Intending to leave, she moved toward the door. "I'll find Tyler Leighton on my own."

Skelly put his arm out to stop her. "All right. I didn't mean to upset you." He sounded sincere when he said, "I'll help you in any way I can. No strings. If you change your mind, though—"

"I won't."

He nodded. "We'll see."

His clipped remark made Keelin think her American cousin was possibly the most cynical man on earth.

Chapter Two

Tyler Leighton was about to enter his building on North Clark Street after a late lunch that he'd barely touched, when he heard the rumble of his name. He glanced over his shoulder to see Nate Feldman, his chief business competitor, rush in his direction after exiting a chauffeured limousine at the corner. In contrast to Feldman's exclusive designer suit, manicured nails and styled hair—or what he had left of it, for he was balding fast—an ever-present cigar was stuck between his thin lips. Tyler hated cigars, which reminded him of lowlifes he'd known.

"Slumming?" Tyler asked, for at a recent social event, he had heard Feldman disparage Tyler's office location to potential customers. Feldman's office was in the Gold Coast, a real-estate ministep up from Lincoln Park West.

Without removing the cigar, the man slurred, "Hey, what sort of greeting is that for an old friend?"

Never, by any stretch of the imagination, would Tyler consider them friends. And he didn't need this aggravation on top of the worry eating at him. The only reason he was working at all was that he couldn't figure out a damn thing he could do personally to get his daughter back. He was working so that he wouldn't go crazy. Not that he was doing a great job of it. He swore that every minute Cheryl was missing took a day off his life.

"What's on your mind, Feldman?"

"I wanted to congratulate you on getting the Uptown job."

Tyler's company, L&O Realty, had recently been awarded the management of a classic movie theater of the thirties that had been boarded up for decades. The renovation would retain its architectural integrity while transforming it into a multiusage arts space. Feldman had bid for the management of it, as well, but had again lost out to Tyler because of his personal vision for the place. And Tyler knew Nate Feldman hated to lose at anything.

"That's big of you," he said, and waited for the man's real motivation in seeking him out.

With a show of exaggeration, Feldman finally removed the cigar and issued a warning. "You won't be so lucky with the North Michigan Avenue project."

Ah, there it was. And some said he was a cynical devil. He merely considered himself realistic. "Do you know something I don't? Or is it some*one*?"

"Maybe I do and maybe I don't," his competitor said with a feral grin. "What *I* have doesn't matter so much, though, when *you're* tied up in that nasty lawsuit over the Wicker Park incident. That changes the balance of things, doesn't it? Let's just say I have the upper hand on this one."

Tightening his jaw—how could Feldman call the death of a kid an *incident?*—Tyler said, "I'm forewarned, then."

"That's the idea."

"But if you don't mind, I'll hold my congratulations until it's a done deal."

"Hold anything you want, for all I care. How about your breath?" Laughing at his own crude humor, Feldman stuck the cigar back in his mouth and signaled the limousine driver. "No holds barred on this one, Leighton. Don't say I didn't warn you."

Tyler didn't wait until the man crept back into his extravagant lair. He immediately entered the first-floor offices of L&O, from which prime real estate was sold and luxury apartments and town houses were rented. He felt all eyes on him as he made his way to the stairs. Worried eyes. Eyes filled with pity.

Cheryl, baby, where are you?

The agonizing question followed him to the second floor, which held his private office, as well as that of his partner, Brock Olander, and their administrative assistants. Brock oversaw the sales and rental parts of the business, while Tyler headed the building-management end. Alma, their receptionist, was nowhere to be seen, and he figured she must be running an errand. He stopped to scan her desk for any messages…anything about his daughter. Nothing. Maybe on *his* desk…

Hopeful, he was on his way to check when he noticed a woman rising from a chair in the waiting area. "Mr. Leighton?"

The soft voice stopped him cold. He gave her a quick once-over—a cloud of shoulder-length dark auburn hair, clear gray eyes, delicate if ordinary features, all of which were unfamiliar to him. All appealing. Something about her spelled *fresh*. Innocent. Maybe the loose flower-print dress that skimmed her slim body, topping ankle boots and bright green cuffed socks. Definitely not professional apparel.

And yet he found himself asking, "Do we have an appointment?" He'd been so distracted since Cheryl disappeared that anything might have slipped his mind.

"No, that we do not. I just took a chance on your seeing me." Drawing closer, she held out her hand and said, "Keelin McKenna."

She spoke with a melodic inflection that was distinctly Irish. Her low voice stirred him for a moment, and he stared, caught by some odd connection, the sensation deepening when their hands clasped. Her gaze meshed with his, and from the surprise he noted in the depths of her eyes, he would swear she noted it, too.

Then reality set in. Cheryl was missing, and his thinking of anything more personal was inappropriate.

Releasing the woman's hand and taking a step back, Tyler said, "I'm sorry. Today's not a good day."

"But I must speak to you," she insisted.

"Ty, there you are." Coming from the stairs, Brock stalked him. "We have to talk. Now."

Mr. Popularity. Suddenly, everyone wanted his attention at the same time. Tyler was oddly relieved by his partner's demand. "All right. In my office." He started to go.

"But, Mr. Leighton—"

Interrupting the woman, he spoke in an impersonal tone even as he kept on walking. "My administrative assistant should be back any minute. Perhaps she can take care of you."

"But it's not her I'm here to see."

He followed Brock inside his office, turning to say, "Then she'll give you an appointment for later in the week."

Please, God, let Cheryl be found by then.

The woman crossed her arms over her chest and raised her chin. "I am not vacating the premises until I've had a word with you about your—"

"Sorry." With regret that went deeper than a fear of being rude, he closed the door in her face and turned to his partner, who seemed reluctant to look him in the eye. That certainly didn't bode well. "Brock, what's the problem?" He was expecting his partner to bring up a new twist in the lawsuit against L&O Realty.

Planting his stocky body directly next to Tyler's massive mahogany desk, Brock muttered, "I know my timing stinks... but I want out." He followed the explosive statement with a deep sigh and ran his hand through his silver-shot hair.

"What?" Tyler stopped short. Surely he misunderstood....

"This has to be a shock, especially now with all you have on your mind. I was planning on telling you a couple of days ago, but then Cheryl disappeared, and it didn't seem like the time—"

Tyler was stunned. He hadn't misunderstood. Brock wanted out of the business. "*This* isn't the time." If ever.

"Yeah, it is. It's actually been a long time in coming." Brock's hazel eyes were steady when he explained, "We're full partners, Ty, but not so that anyone would know it. When someone mentions L&O Realty, people think of you."

Their partnership hadn't started out that way, but Tyler had always had more drive than his laid-back partner, and their present roles had evolved over the years. Brock had never before complained.

"So this is about ego?" Tyler asked.

"It's way beyond something so simple." Brock seemed almost regretful as he explained, "I'm tired of being pigeonholed. Unappreciated."

"I appreciate the hell out of you, Brock."

"Only because I do the work that doesn't interest you anymore. You can focus on redeveloping buildings—redeveloping dreams—while I handle the boring day-to-day details of rentals and sales."

Tyler felt as if he'd been blindsided. How had he missed this? He couldn't conceive of their decade-long partnership ending without warning.

"If you've been dissatisfied, why haven't you said something before?"

"I've tried in a dozen different ways. Maybe not directly enough... Why couldn't you have been listening?"

Not the first time he'd been accused of being so focused on his own goals and desires that he couldn't recognize someone else's needs. Guilt rocked him. He regretted that he'd failed the man with whom he'd built his success. Surely it wasn't too late.

"Look, Brock, give me some time, would you? I'm not all here right now, but I know I don't want this to happen. And I hope you don't really, either. If we put our heads together, we can work things out. I promise I'll try to give you whatever it is you need."

Tyler moved around him, planted himself before a window overlooking Lincoln Park. Arms crossed over his chest, he stared out at the lush trees and flower beds near the south pond with unseeing eyes. Everything seemed to be caving in on him. The accident at the Wicker Park site. The lawsuit. His daughter. Feldman. Now this.

"All I can concentrate on right now is Cheryl," he said, trying to forget the rest.

"You know how much I love your girl. She calls me Uncle Brock, for crissakes."

Desperate, Tyler thought of something that might make Brock feel more needed while taking a worry off his shoulders. He turned to face the partner he didn't want to lose.

"Listen, Brock, Nate Feldman's breathing down my neck about the North Michigan Avenue project. You could take over for me."

"Feldman?" A pregnant pause was followed by Brock's careful, "What do you think he's up to?"

"Probably something devious."

"Hell!" Brock's tense expression intensified.

"Put this idea of splitting on hold, would you, Brock? At least until I find Cheryl."

At the mention of his daughter's name, the door burst open and his assistant, Pamela Redmond, ran into his office so fast the chestnut topknot she wore to make her look taller threatened to topple. "'The Whole Story,'" she gasped, clearly out of breath as if she'd run straight up the stairs. "Channel 8!"

Tyler retrieved the remote control and turned on the television in the wall unit to see his own face staring back at him.

"Cheryl wouldn't have run away. She had no reason. She was a happy kid. A normal kid. She wasn't involved in gangs or drugs. We had a great relationship. We never even fought."

He lowered the sound as the anchor's voice-over continued with speculation about the case.

"That was supposed to be hard-news footage, for God's sake!" He couldn't take his eyes off the screen, off the image of his missing daughter. "I'd be furious that some electronic rag is bandying around my personal life if I weren't so worried about Cheryl."

"Right. Think of the positive," Pamela said, her dark eyes melting with concern. "Maybe this piece will alert someone who's seen her... like that missing-persons program."

"I hope so. I'd be thankful for anything that'd bring her back."

Tyler only hoped the producers of the tabloid show wouldn't continue to follow up certain nuances of the story... like an investigation into Cheryl's mother's death....

"Listen, Ty," Brock said, his agitation clearly growing. "I'm sorry this is all hitting you at once, but you're going to have to deal with my wanting out. Soon."

Realizing a commercial filled the screen, Tyler shut off the television. "We'll talk about it after Cheryl is safe." The look he gave his partner pleaded with him not to object.

His square jaw tightening, bobbing his head in agreement, Brock turned toward the door.

"You can leave, as well, Pamela," Tyler said, feeling the need to brood in solitude for a while.

His assistant backed off but said, "There's a woman who's been waiting to see you. A Keelin McKenna."

Envisioning a cloud of auburn hair and clear gray eyes, he muttered, "She's still here? Get rid of her. Nicely, of course."

"You will not be rid of me just yet," came a soft, lilting reply from the doorway.

He started as the Irishwoman entered his office uninvited. "Now, see here—"

"You just said that you would be thankful for anything that might help bring back your daughter."

His gut tensed. "What about Cheryl?"

"Uh, I have some work to do," Pamela said, retreating. "I'll just leave you two alone."

The door closed and Tyler stared at Miss Keelin McKenna. "I'm waiting."

"A seat?" she murmured as if he'd offered her one. "Why, yes, thank you." Then she crossed to the couch and three upholstered chairs set around a heavy coffee table.

"So sit already and spill." When her forehead creased as if in puzzlement, he said, "Talk. What do you know about my daughter's whereabouts?"

She sank into one of the chairs. "I wish I *could* tell you where to find her."

"So you don't know, after all." He stalked her, towered over her, hoped to intimidate her into telling the truth. "Then why are you wasting my time?"

"Because I might be able to help puzzle it out."

He narrowed his gaze on the woman. His antennae went on alert and rightly so. He wasn't a man who suffered fools easily. And he was used to people coming to him with hare-brained schemes in hopes of separating him from some of his money.

"So how much do you want? For your help?"

She shook her head. "I have no interest in monetary payment, Mr. Leighton."

"What, then?"

"My reasons are personal."

"Which obviously you aren't going to share."

If he thought he could goad her into slipping, he was wrong. Her gaze steady, she waited. For his permission to continue? He sat and gestured for her to go on.

Keelin took a deep breath. "I have rather unusual dreams. Not dreams, really. More like visions that come to me while I sleep." Her tongue darted to wet her lips as if she were having trouble getting the words out. "I see through other people's eyes... know their thoughts... as if I'm inside their heads."

Great. A kook. Any hope he might have had dashed, he indicated the door. "You're wasting my time."

She didn't budge. "I've seen through your daughter's eyes twice, Mr. Leighton. First, when she ran away and—"

"Cheryl didn't have any reason to run away!"

She continued, "And the second time, when someone found her."

The skin at the back of his neck crawled. What was wrong with him? He didn't believe in ESP or whatever this was. He didn't believe *her* and a story that was too preposterous for words.

"Look, you've got the wrong man. Give it up."

"You live in a huge home on the lake and opposite a ravine," she went on calmly, as if he hadn't spoken.

"Which you undoubtedly saw in a news clip."

"Your daughter's bedroom overlooks the water." Her expression turned inward as if she were remembering. When she said, "One of the steps in the front staircase creaks," he felt a chill shoot down his spine.

Still, he said, "That step has needed fixing for years. Anyone familiar with the house could have told you that."

"A pedestal in the foyer supports an unusual sculpture that reminds Cheryl of an angel about to take flight."

His pulse surged. The sculpture was new. Not many people had seen it yet. And Cheryl *had* told him it reminded her of an angel. . . .

"I almost forgot. You keep emergency money in your study. Tens and twenties. She took them all."

That did it. Tyler lunged to his feet. "How the hell could you have known what I didn't tell anyone but the police?" he demanded, wondering if his daughter's taking the emergency-cash fund had somehow become common knowledge, more fodder for people bored with their own lives.

Her steady gray gaze turned up to him. "I saw."

"You *saw* Cheryl take the money."

"Not in the same way as if I were watching a movie, no. I saw the bills . . . her hands . . . the leather wallet. It's as if I was inside her." She squeezed her eyes shut for a second. "As if I *was* her for a few minutes."

He dropped back to the couch and stared as her lids drifted back open. He didn't know what to make of Keelin McKenna. She couldn't be telling the truth. Her story played out like bestselling fiction. He was dealing with reality here. His fourteen-year-old daughter was missing.

What to do?

Tyler was torn. Either this woman really did know something about Cheryl's disappearance or she had an in with one of the policemen who had given her details no one else was privy to. Maybe he'd better check

that out, and while he was at it, he could get the police to check *her* out. Maybe she was in on the kidnapping. Maybe that's why he hadn't gotten a ransom
note—because she was going to work him somehow.

"I need some time to think," he said.

"I fear time is running out."

He ignored the renewed prickling at his nape. "Why
don't you give me your address and phone number so
I can get in touch with you?"

Looking crestfallen, she answered, "I'm staying at
the Hotel Clareton."

"The hotel?"

"I just flew in from Cork early this morning."

He was startled. "Then you weren't even here when
Cheryl disappeared."

"No." Her smooth brow furrowed. "I don't understand it, either—a stranger in a strange land. No
connection between us. I knew the others."

Despite his well-cultivated cynicism, he wanted to
believe her. At the same time, her sucking him in made
him uneasy. He was a rational man, one not given to
being conned. What was it about this woman that got
to him where he lived? He was vulnerable because of
Cheryl, he reminded himself, because the only person
who really meant anything to him was missing. If
anything happened to her, it would kill him. And
Keelin McKenna could use his powerful emotions
against him.

As if reading his thoughts, she pressed her case.
"You say you would do anything to find your daughter."

"I would."

He'd done questionable things to protect Cheryl
over the years, but his efforts hadn't been sharp

enough. They'd been too narrow. Danger had come from an unexpected direction.

"Then trust me," Keelin pleaded, her tone heartfelt. "I do not know your city—therefore, I cannot find her alone."

What would it hurt? He was in a no-win position. He'd get Pamela to contact both the police and his private detective to see what they could come up with on Keelin McKenna. In the meantime, he'd become her shadow.

"All right," he said. "I'm willing to give you the benefit of the doubt. For Cheryl's sake."

"Good."

Her relieved smile mesmerized him. It trembled on her lips, lent a sheen to her eyes, brushed a glow across her cheeks. Like a quiet little bud blooming into a full-blown flower, Keelin suddenly appeared unspeakably beautiful. Again, he felt the connection . . . and purposely stood and turned his back on her to break it. He couldn't let her affect him in any way. He needed his wits about him, needed to concentrate on what was important here.

"You can tell me more about these powers of yours over dinner," he said. "And you'll detail the *dreams* concerning my daughter. Maybe I can pick up on something you couldn't."

"That was my thought."

Or he'd trick her into revealing her hand, he added to himself.

Suddenly, the appetite that had eluded him at lunch kicked in. He felt not only a powerful hunger, but also a renewed strength that had eluded him for the past two days. He was energized by doing, and his allowing others to handle things had festered inside him.

If the woman had the power to make some other-worldly connection with his daughter, then she'd make a believer of him. And if she had had anything to do with the girl's disappearance...she would be damn sorry.

If Keelin McKenna were part of some con to wring money out of him at the expense of his daughter, he would personally turn her life into a living hell.

NEARLY AN HOUR LATER, still waiting for Tyler Leighton to finish up business, Keelin wondered if she'd made a pact with the devil—a dark-haired, pale-eyed, too-handsome devil. She knew he didn't trust her, and she could hardly blame him.

But he had agreed, and that's all that counted.

This time, the story would end well, she assured herself. They'd find Cheryl Leighton, and from that day forward, her father would keep her safe. Keelin had no doubts as to his love for and devotion to his daughter. She didn't know what had driven Cheryl to run, though she gathered the girl blamed him for some terrible lie.

A misunderstanding, perhaps?

Keelin rested her head against the chair back, her energy suddenly at a low. The dreams had interfered with her sleep the past two nights. Added to jet lag...

"I'm ready."

Her eyes quickly opened. "And just as I was getting comfortable." She forced herself from the chair and into close proximity of Tyler Leighton. Too close. His warmth reached out to her, curled along her tired body.

"I wouldn't get too comfortable around me if I were you," he murmured.

"A warning?"

"Call it what you will."

She stared up at his enigmatic expression. Though she was of average height and size, she felt dwarfed by the man. He wasn't so very tall—she judged him to be just short of six feet. And he wasn't so very large—his shoulders were of medium breadth beneath his tailored suit jacket. But she recognized strength in his face and power in his gaze when he stared at her with his lids half-lowered as if he were trying to sear her brain.

She suspected she *should* be a bit afraid of the man, but at the moment, she was too weary even to be intimidated. "Then I'll consider it a challenge," she finally returned. "But don't underestimate me, Mr. Leighton. I'm as motivated as you are to find your daughter." In some ways, more so. She had a lot to make up for.

"Then let's get started. And my name is Tyler."

She found *Mr. Leighton* safer, not that she would admit it. As he held the office door open for her, she nodded agreeably and adopted a positive attitude.

Seeing to Cheryl Leighton's safety wouldn't bring back Gavin Daley, but it might assuage a bit of her guilt, Keelin thought hopefully as they descended to the first floor. Besides, she certainly didn't need another soul on her conscience.

Downstairs, she waited in the sheltered entryway while Tyler left her to fetch his vehicle from the car park across the street. A movement to her right caught her eye. Her attention refocused, she watched a stocky man slide out from the protection of a nearby doorway. Middle-aged, with a jowly face and salt-and-pepper hair, the man glanced around furtively, then crossed the street at a trot, entering the same door that Tyler had taken.

She frowned and her stomach tightened for a moment until a bottle green Jaguar rolled out through the car-park exit and stopped directly across the street from her. Tyler swung open the car door and slid from behind the wheel, then motioned for her to cross.

A quick look around assured her there was no sign of the other man. Undoubtedly, he was merely fetching his car, as well, she decided. Shaking away the odd feeling his furtive actions had given her, she waited for a break in traffic, then raced to the car.

Tyler drove in silence, toward the center of the city, stopping at a lovely two-story restaurant. A doorman opened her car door, and as she stepped out, a valet traded places with Tyler, who then escorted her inside, where glass walls provided a splendid view of the river. The tables were draped with white linen, their centers decorated with bouquets of fresh cut flowers mixed with herbs.

Taking pleasure where she could, Keelin inhaled the fragrance and absorbed the ambiance. She was certain she wasn't going to enjoy what was coming. Tensely, she waited for the inquisition.

It seemed as though Tyler was in no hurry. They perused menus and ordered. The waiter quickly brought a bottle of merlot, and after Tyler approved it, filled two stemmed glasses. Keelin sipped at the red wine. As tired as she was, one glass would be her limit, or Tyler would have to carry her out of the restaurant. The wine was relaxing her when he finally got down to business.

"So tell me about this unusual ability of yours."

"I dream through other people's eyes," she told him again. "I cannot explain it any more accurately."

"So in your dream, you see what someone else, who is awake, is seeing at that very moment?" When she nodded, he asked, "How long has this been going on?"

"Always, I guess. When I was young, I simply thought all my dreams were normal, and as I began to sort out the difference between real dreams and these...visions...I assumed everyone had similar experiences. Then I learned that no one else in my family had the...well, gift or curse, however you want to think of it. Except Gran, of course. My father's mother, Moira. She explained things to me."

The way Tyler was looking at her, she couldn't tell if he believed her.

"And what exactly did she tell you?"

"That I was given a responsibility which I couldn't put aside. That I was the one to inherit this gift because I was strong enough to deal with the consequences."

Not that she *felt* strong. If she could give the supposed gift away, she'd do it in a heartbeat, just as she'd told her grandmother at age fifteen—after the first of the darker episodes that she called her night terrors.

Always a wise woman, Moira had merely said a person couldn't fight her fate. It had taken more than a decade and an unnecessary death to convince Keelin of it.

After the waiter had delivered their salads and a basket of bread, Tyler continued his line of questioning. "What kind of consequences?"

Not about to share her personal traumas with a stranger, she made light of the issue. "Having to deal with the distrustful sort who thinks I make my living spinning fairy tales.'' She punctuated the observation with a forkful of salad and a piece of crusty bread. Both were delicious.

But Tyler didn't seem about to let her off the hook with a joke. "How *do* you make your living?"

"Herbs."

"What? You grow or sell them for cooking?"

"And for healing."

His dark eyebrows shot up at that one. She was used to skepticism when it came to alternative therapies. She wasn't about to try to convince him that many modern medicines were based on herbal remedies.

"So was it herbs that brought you here from Ireland? Or was it Cheryl?"

Relieved he wasn't going to take issue with her work, but not missing the shot about his daughter, she said, "Actually, I'm here to see family. My father's sister and brother both emigrated to the United States more than three decades ago." She figured if she was being honest, she might as well go all the way. Taking a big breath, she said, "Skelly McKenna is my first cousin."

He shrugged. "Am I supposed to know who he is?"

"You do in a way." Her fingers tightened on the stem of her glass. "You watched his telecast this afternoon."

" 'The Whole Story?' "

"That would be the one."

"What the hell? Is that why you sought me out?" His roar turned heads. "To get a story for a TV rag?"

Embarrassed by the unwanted attention, she shrank into her seat. "No, of course not. I told you why. Skelly's doing the story on your daughter's disappearance was coincidence.'' From his glare, she didn't figure he believed her, but she went on. ''It was how I recognized her.''

He lowered his voice. ''I thought you were inside her. That you didn't see her. Or did Cheryl conveniently look at herself in a mirror on the way out of our house?''

Keelin shook her head. ''I had no idea what she looked like until a few hours ago. The bracelet—the strands of leather with magical charms. I saw it on her wrist in my dreams and then again on the studio monitor while I was waiting for Skelly. That's how I put it together. I had no idea of who the girl in my head was until that moment, I swear.''

Tyler appeared to be bursting with accusations or questions—she didn't know which—but the waiter's serving their meals held either off.

Keelin didn't have much success eating her pasta creation, which was bursting with fresh, barely cooked vegetables and judiciously sprinkled herbs. Tyler, however, wolfed down his rare steak like a man possessed. Tension sizzled along her nerves. She hated the feeling. Unlike her more easily inflamed sister, Flanna, she wasn't one to thrive on arguments and stress. If she had a choice, she would pick herself up and walk away from this whole situation and never look back.

But she had no choice. She had Cheryl Leighton to find.

''Why are you doing this?'' Tyler suddenly asked.

''A fourteen-year-old girl is in trouble.'' And she couldn't—wouldn't—turn her back on the daughter, no matter how the father felt about her.

''You said something about personal reasons before.''

"Yes, I did."

"If you want me to believe you, you'll have to tell me more. Be totally honest."

Lies. All lies . . .

Why did he do it? Why? Now that I know, everything is ruined.

Keelin's head spun with the remembered fragments of her dreams. Cheryl had to have been thinking of her father. Who else?

Careful as to how she framed her response, she asked, "Have you always been so honest? Would you reveal every detail of yourself to anyone who would ask? For that fact, would you be completely truthful even with your own daughter?"

Tyler's complexion paled. She'd definitely hit a raw nerve. His skin appeared almost gray, she thought, realizing she was far from happy for hitting her mark. Her discomfort grew when his gaze meshed with hers and she recognized the pain that went deeper than his eyes, perhaps all the way to his soul. She had intimate knowledge of that kind of pain, and she respected its right to remain private.

Chagrined, she said, "I'm sorry."

Slowly, he nodded. "But you had a point."

"I wish you could take me on faith."

"Let's say I continue to give you the benefit of my doubt."

"As long as that means I don't have to do this on my own."

He sat back and stared. "I don't get you."

"You needn't."

She could tell Tyler Leighton didn't particularly like puzzles, especially ones he couldn't solve. She guessed he was a man who would pick away until he came up with a solution. Hopefully, she wouldn't be around him long enough for him to lay her open.

"Let me tell you about the dreams," she suggested, and spent the next quarter of an hour replaying them both to the best of her ability, giving Tyler every visual detail she remembered.

She held back Cheryl's thoughts because she didn't want to sound accusatory, and she didn't want to sharpen his pain. Besides, whatever had happened between father and daughter, he already knew. And it was none of her business. Tyler and Cheryl would have to work on the reasons for her running away *after* they found her.

"Who could she have been meeting at the concert?" Tyler murmured once she fell silent.

"I never saw the person. That's when I awoke."

"Maybe one of her friends."

"Have you spoken to them?"

"The police have tracked down her school friends, as well as ones in the neighborhood. And the private detective I hired did the same. They came up with zero."

"Who does Cheryl know in the city?"

He shrugged. "Beats me."

"Does she have an address book at home?"

"I'm not sure . . . but we can look for one. Good thinking."

"If she were thinking straight, darling, she wouldn't be here with you, now, would she?" a carefully modulated if throaty voice countered.

To Keelin's amazement, an elegant blonde in a clingy summer sheath appeared at their table. She was stunning and perfectly groomed, as if she'd just stepped out of an exclusive salon. A thick gold necklace and several rings with large stones attested to her wealth.

"Vivian," Tyler muttered as if her name were a curse.

The luscious Vivian gave a speechless Keelin a once-over. "A bit unsophisticated for your taste, isn't she, Tyler?"

"And you're as rude as ever, Vivian."

She batted long lashes over intensely green eyes. "You didn't always think so...and not so long ago, I might add," she purred, running long, French-manicured fingernails under his chin.

Tyler ducked his head away from her touch. "Don't make a scene. Whoever you're with must be waiting for you."

"Yes, he is, thank you." She turned to Keelin. "And you, darling, a little friendly warning between us girls. Be on guard. Tyler Leighton takes no prisoners. He'll break your poor heart if you let him. Ta."

With a wave of her beringed hand, she was gone, leaving Keelin stunned and with heat climbing her neck.

She was more than thankful when Tyler ignored her discomfort, casually saying, "If you're done eating, I'll take you over to Grant Park, to the band shell."

The last place she'd seen Cheryl in her dream.

Chapter Three

As he aimed the Jaguar for Grant Park, the band-shell area being barely a mile from the restaurant, Tyler was aware of exactly how much Vivian Claiborne had flustered Keelin. While she could be the most engaging creature on earth, when angry, Vivian could also be a nasty piece of work. He'd quickly grown tired of her razor-sharp tongue. Besides, he'd suspected she had her sights on him to be husband number three. One marriage to a woman more interested in what he had than who he was as a person had been enough. He'd gladly broken off his short-lived relationship with Vivian before it could get out of hand.

Unfortunately, Vivian was a woman who didn't take even the slightest of rejections well.

And she'd definitely managed to subdue Keelin. The Irishwoman sat in silence, her attention fixed on whatever flew by the passenger-side window. He let her alone, figuring she would recover quickly enough once they arrived.

The band shell was not in use tonight, so the area was dark and fairly deserted. Even so, a few blocks away, the Buckingham Fountain's color display added to the lure of the lakeshore and drew myriad visitors, so finding an available parking meter was out of the question. He pulled the car into a no-parking zone a few hundred yards from the band shell and cut the engine.

"Parking here isn't legal," Keelin murmured.

"I noticed. I break the rules when I have to," he said grimly. "C'mon. Get out. I doubt we'll be here long enough for it to make a difference anyway."

By the time he circled to the sidewalk, she was out of the car, facing west, taking in the electric skyline looming over Michigan Avenue. He closed the door and stared at her features, garishly illuminated by the streetlights. Her eyes were wide, her lips parted, and a visible pulse throbbed in her slender throat. She was caught. And for the moment, he was caught by her.

What was going through that head of hers? Did she recognize the area or was she trying to make him think she did? Cynic that he was, he knew it would take more than her word to make him believe her.

"This is it," she finally murmured. "I recognize everything. The position of the buildings. The lit signs. The bridge she took to get to the band shell."

He focused on Monroe Street near the Art Institute. A homeless man had stationed himself on one side of the bridge. A couple of punks were play-streetfighting on the other side. The kind of people his daughter had been forced to deal with? He didn't know that, he reminded himself, trying to remain calm. He still wasn't convinced that Cheryl had been on her own. If he believed she was, then he would have to believe she had run away from him. He would have to believe her disappearance was *his* fault.

The suggestion made him gruff. "Getting any good vibes?"

Keelin's eyes narrowed as they met his. "Let's walk around the band shell. Maybe I'll pick some up."

He didn't miss her sarcastic tone. He took her arm and escorted her onto the lawn. She was silent but for the small breaths and sighs she occasionally released as she gazed around the area seeming able to see through the thickening dark. Suddenly, she stopped dead and faced the band shell, her arm trembling under his hand. Instinctively, he released her.

She glanced to her right, her eyes narrowing as if she were measuring. She stepped several yards back and to her left. Adjusting. She checked herself and corrected her position again. Finally satisfied, she nodded. "Here."

"Here, what?"

"Where Cheryl waited, afraid and trying to concentrate on the music. Liszt. A piece *you* listen to." Frowning, she faced him. "She was upset because it reminded her of you."

His hair prickled at the back of his neck. "Why didn't you tell me this before?"

As if she hadn't heard him, she sank to the lawn, concentrating. The prickling spread down his spine when she cocked her head and glanced over her shoulder, pointing. "The voice came from over there somewhere."

He stared in the direction she indicated, hoping to see something, feel something. Of course, he didn't.

"The voice startled her," Keelin went on, as if in a trance, "and she jerked around...."

She sat very still for a moment, obviously concentrating, her expression changing slightly as if she remembered something. Then she swept her hands through the grass.

"What?"

"Something flew out of her fingers onto the ground."

Right. "And the clean-up crew would have found whatever that was."

Keelin would know that, he told himself. She was merely playacting for effect. Still, he tensely watched her as she continued to examine the ground around her, getting to her knees and widening her search. He fought the urge to drop to his knees and help, fought making a damn fool of himself.

Still, his gut tightened when she murmured, "Wait . . . I think I felt something."

Her fingers scrabbled, digging through the green blades. When her hand whipped up, something small was clasped tightly between two fingers. Quickly, she rose to her feet and came to his side.

He held out his hand, and Keelin placed the object in his palm. A chill shot through him. Even in the near-dark, he recognized it. A fairy charm from the bracelet his daughter always wore.

He remembered Cheryl's complaining that he hadn't been spending enough time with her last summer, that he was too busy with his work. He'd tried making up for his negligence. They'd spent an entire weekend together, Sunday at the Renaissance Fair. They'd had a great time, an unforgettable day, just the two of them. The bracelet had been outrageously priced for scraps of leather and small bits of metal, but he'd seen how his daughter's eyes shone when she'd looked at it, and he hadn't been able to resist buying it for her. The bracelet was her prized possession, and she rarely removed it.

Keelin's eyes were shining when she asked, "Now do you believe me?"

"I believe you know something about Cheryl," he agreed, the proof in his hand. "What I don't know is if you're telling the truth about these dreams of yours."

"But the charm—"

He slipped it in his pocket. "Could have been planted. Or you could have had it all along, palmed it, pretended to have found it." He loomed over her and grabbed her upper arms, wishing he could wring the truth from her. "Did you have anything to do with my daughter's disappearance?"

The excited light extinguished from her eyes, she said, "No!" and pulled her arms free, one at a time. Her face saddened by disappointment and disgust, she turned her back on him and marched across the lawn.

He lost no time in following. "Where do you think you're going?"

"To my hotel."

"What about my daughter?"

"What about her?" She stopped and faced him. "What truth did she learn that was so devastating that she ran from you?"

"I don't know what you're talking about." But deep in his heart, he was beginning to fear he might.

"At this moment, is anything more important to you than your daughter's safety?"

"Nothing." She was his whole life. If anything happened to her...

"Then prove it. Take some responsibility and stop placing the blame."

His "All right" seemed to take her off guard. She blinked and sucked in her breath.

"Suddenly, you believe me?" she asked quietly. "Just like that?"

He couldn't say the words. "I'll stop placing the blame," he promised instead.

Whether she was innocent or guilty, he sensed Keelin would lead him to his daughter. In the long run, bringing Cheryl home safe was all that mattered to him.

"So what have we accomplished by coming here?" he asked. "Other than your treading the path in your dream?"

"It makes the connection real for me. I hoped to see something I missed earlier...but I didn't. Still, it makes tangible what I knew in my heart. I wish it did for you, as well," she said, her tone fervent.

He held fast to his distrust. "Nothing more? No indications of who might have found Cheryl? What the person looked like, for instance?"

"I'm not a psychic," she protested. "At least, not in the way you're suggesting. I can't make predictions. I can't usually envision places or people I haven't *seen* through physical contact, so I'm not quite sure how it was I ended up seeing Cheryl in my dreams. Most of the time I experience real events and emotions through dreams. That's it."

Keelin rubbed a lethargic hand across her forehead, and he responded in kind despite his agitation. She looked exhausted, as if she could hardly stay on her feet, and there was a fragility about her that he hadn't noticed before. Not physically, perhaps, but of spirit.

"Perhaps I'd better get you to your hotel."

Keelin sighed wearily. "I could use some sleep."

"And maybe you'll dream again."

"I cannot force it," she warned him.

"I'll take my chances."

Including the opportunity to talk further with this mysterious woman. If there was one thing he knew how to do, it was to make the opposite sex open up to him.

He determined that whatever her game, Keelin McKenna would be no exception.

ON THE SHORT RIDE HOME, Keelin couldn't rid herself of the bitter aftertaste Tyler Leighton provoked. He'd brought up all the old insecurities. The feeling of helplessness. Of being thought a liar or a fool. She couldn't blame him, she supposed, and yet it was difficult to be generous toward him when all she was trying to do was help his daughter.

If only she could have done this alone.

The Hotel Clareton, tucked on a side street of the Gold Coast, blended perfectly with other limestone and brownstone buildings surrounding it. Elegant yet understated, the modest establishment offered all the amenities of a larger hotel, with even more personal service.

Swinging open the Jaguar's passenger door, the liveried doorman said, "Miss McKenna, I trust you're having a good evening."

She forced a smile and let the polite inquiry hang.

"Take care of the car," Tyler said, handing the man a large bill.

"Certainly." The doorman motioned for a younger uniformed man to come forward and move the Jaguar.

In a low voice, she said, "No reason you need to see me to my room."

When Tyler insisted, "Of course there is," she had the distinct feeling that he meant to do more than escort her to her suite and leave. Not wanting to argue the point before the hotel's employees, she spun on her heel and through the hotel's entry.

Tyler followed her inside, past a lobby decorated in champagne and gold with touches of palest pink. Her suite was decorated in similar fashion, the sofa and two chairs in her sitting room identical to those in the lobby. The walls were a subdued pink with a gold sheen, warming the flawlessly appointed setting. And the coffee table held a spray of matching pink tiger lilies, as did the chest in the bedroom. When he stepped inside, she noted Tyler's raised eyebrows and assumed he was calculating the expense.

Trying to be subtle, she said, "I really am very tired."

"I imagine you are," he said, continuing to wander through her temporary living quarters.

All right, so she had to be more direct. "I'm trying to end the evening."

"Consider it ended." He dropped onto the sofa.

She shut the door so their words wouldn't echo down the hall. "Not with you here."

While she was willing to put up with the man for his child's sake, she wouldn't allow him to get too close for her own. He kept prying under her skin, poking and prodding at her innermost being. Knowing he had secrets of his own, she suspected he was exactly the type of man who could get what he wanted from her if he kept at it.

The type of man she made a point of avoiding.

"I'm not going," he stated.

Fearing the consequences if she didn't set boundaries, she drew closer to him and crossed her arms over her chest. "You cannot stay in my rooms."

"You certainly can't expect me to drive back to North Bluff. If you have one of your *visionary* dreams, it would take me better than a half hour to get back here, even in the middle of the night. Then how would we get to Cheryl in time?"

Unable to miss his sarcasm even as he made a sensible point, she settled into a high-backed chair opposite him. "So what are you proposing?"

"That I spend the night on your sofa. Don't worry, I have no desire to invade your bedroom."

"That never occurred to me," she hedged, the vision clear in her mind the moment he put words to it.

"No?" His eyebrows lifted fractionally, as if he knew better. "You seem tense." He looked around the room, his gaze settling on a drink cart. "A little brandy would do us both good."

Did he hope liquor would loosen her up, or loosen up her tongue? She thought the latter. Let him try. He couldn't wring from her a truth he suspected she was hiding, not when she was innocent of any wrongdoing.

While he decanted the brandy, the red glow on her telephone finally caught her eye. Realizing a message awaited her, she picked up the receiver, read the instructions and punched in the code to retrieve it. So many technical advances in this America of her relatives . . . and her used to a far more simple life.

"Hey, cuz, Skelly here. Call me first thing in the morning, would you? I've got some info on Tyler Leighton that I think you need to know."

A beep was followed by an electronic voice telling her she had no more messages.

What could her cousin have learned about Tyler? she wondered. Something she needed to know . . . and Skelly's tone had seemed a bit ominous.

She hung up just as Tyler made himself comfortable on the sofa and handed her a glass.

"Who was that?"

"My cousin. Family business."

Feeling the heat creep up her neck, she cursed her inability to tell the smallest of untruths without telegraphing the fact. But if Tyler noticed the flush spreading up into her face, he didn't say a word. His expression blank—purposely so? she wondered—he seemed content in his silence until her glass was half-empty.

"So why don't you make an effort to convince me?" he finally suggested.

He didn't have to be more specific. She knew he was referring to her ability. "I'm not certain that I can."

"Me, neither, but you can start with whatever you're holding back," he suggested, "with what makes finding Cheryl so important to you."

"I doubt anything I tell you will change your mind."

"Try me."

Tyler sounded as if he were serious. And the way he was looking at her—as if he were *afraid* to trust her—touched Keelin. Sensing he meant what he said, that he really wanted to be convinced, she didn't see any harm in relating the first part of the story.

"After Gran explained everything to me," she began, "I hated the fact that I was different. But I couldn't change things, couldn't run away from who

I was. I felt the huge responsibility she spoke of in my heart and in my soul."

"How old were you?"

"Fifteen."

"Not much older than Cheryl. Heavy stuff for a kid . . ."

She could almost hear him mentally adding *If it's true.*

"The dreams always sprang from strong emotions," she went on. "Sometimes good emotions, sometimes bad, but always very, very intense."

"And the bad ones upset you?"

Keelin nodded. "Of course, though they weren't anything of great significance until . . ." She took another sip of her brandy for courage. Sharing this still wasn't easy. "My closest chum was a schoolmate. Deirdre Flanagan. One night, I saw her being molested—I *felt* her being molested and fighting a boy we both knew. I woke up near-hysterical, made Da ring the constable. I was certain I was reporting a crime in progress." The painful memories washed over her. "When they were caught together, Deirdre told the constable that Tully O'Meara was her new boyfriend and that he hadn't done anything she hadn't wanted." She took a deep breath. "Afterward, she and my other schoolmates froze me out for telling."

"But even if you were wrong, you were trying to help her."

"And I'm not certain that I wasn't correct. In my heart, I believe that Deirdre was raped . . . but I suppose she thought admitting to it would stigmatize her more than if people merely thought she fell from the virtuous path."

"So she lied to save face."

"And in so doing made me an outcast. A subject of jest. This from a good friend," she said sadly, remembering as if the betrayal had just happened. "I wanted to die of embarrassment."

"Being a social outcast as a teenager would be traumatic," Tyler admitted. "But if you're saying that's your motivation, the reason that you've got to find Cheryl—"

"No."

After abruptly cutting him off, Keelin splashed back the last of her brandy and reveled in the smooth burn of the liquor sliding down her throat. This is what she *could not* speak of. What she had never told anyone but her confessor. The burden she'd carried around with her. The guilt she could never wash away completely. Day after day, year after year, she'd thought it impossible to redeem herself.

But maybe she'd been wrong.

Maybe finding Cheryl Leighton before something terrible happened to the girl was her chance at last.

She set down the empty glass on the table next to her. "I'm saying 'tis the reason that, for many years, I chose to ignore the ability I inherited from my grandmother. And there were terrible consequences to be paid." An image of Gavin Daley's body caught in the shallows of Lough Danaan danced in her head. Her eyes stung with the vision that haunted her. "I cannot let that happen again."

"So exactly what was it that happened?"

"That's all I'll be telling you," she insisted, bouncing up from her chair, head down so he wouldn't see the tears trembling on her lids.

Tyler was equally quick. Before she could get around him, he'd blocked her path, and his hands were encasing her arms again. "Tell me."

"No!" Her refusal was a ragged cry.

"I think you need to talk about it."

Slowly, she raised her head, forced herself to look at him. Her pulse surged. What she saw etched in his features startled her. Empathy. Concern. For her?

But it couldn't be.

"What do you care about my needs?" she asked softly, aware of his fingers burning into her flesh. "You think I'm a fraud. That I am out to trick you of your precious money. Not everyone is motivated by greed."

The sensation spread, making her want to move closer, to feel his arms around her. She needed succor, and yet she could not ask for it, because she could not be totally honest.

"Experience tells me different."

"I live a comfortable life, and that's enough for me. Can you say the same?" With that, she shrugged free and tore into her bedroom. "You can see yourself out."

She slammed the bedroom door and locked it, then threw herself across the four-poster bed. She fisted the pink satin quilt and squeezed, willed herself not to cry. Too many tears already. Her heart was hammering in her breast so hard she thought she might be sick.

She hadn't meant to defend herself. But that's what she had done, had nearly pleaded for Tyler's trust. Why? He didn't have to trust her. He only had to go along with her. She knew that. And also knew she wanted more.

This made no sense, this connection she'd felt from the moment he'd faced her in his office, this charged undercurrent between them that swayed and dipped and suddenly rushed over her with frightening intensity. Simply stated, Tyler Leighton made her uncomfortable.

He was too complex, too powerful, and something inside him was too dark.

She should have backed off the moment she sensed the danger, and yet, instead, she'd come closer like a moth to the flame. Despite his distrust of her, she was drawn to him. As he was to her, she realized.

What was wrong with her? she wondered. Why had she suddenly lost her good sense? She'd spent her adulthood on guard. Setting boundaries. Maintaining emotional distances. Keeping herself safe.

She could continue to do so if she tried, Keelin assured herself. If only she weren't so exhausted. Lack of rest had lowered her defenses, perhaps even made her imagine untruths. She didn't have to succumb.

Not to Tyler Leighton.

All she needed to regain her normal control was a good, deep sleep....

AFTER TOSSING AND TURNING in the lumpy bed for hours, she gave up on falling asleep. She was creeped out anyway after seeing the rat on the back porch when she'd put the garbage out. Faint street light shone in through the single window. The narrow, sparsely furnished room looked better in the near-dark, she decided. Nothing like her room at home, of course, but in the circumstances, it would do.

Better than the streets.

Still, she felt spooked again. Maybe she could fall asleep on the couch watching TV. She rose from the bed and crossed the room, stopping before the door when she heard raised voices on the other side.

"How long are we going to wait?"

"Until I say."

Wait for what?

She shifted from one bare foot to the other, fingered one of the charms on her bracelet. A sudden breeze from the open window crawled up her bare legs, all the way up to the hem of her T-shirt. Shivering, she pressed her ear to the door.

"You're forgetting who's in charge here."

"In charge?"

"All right. Maybe that's a little strong. But it was my idea."

"True enough. You want a medal?"

"No, I just want to write the damn ransom note and get it over with."

Ransom note?

She knew what that was. She'd watched enough TV, seen enough movies. But what were they talking about? They hadn't kidnapped her or anything. She'd agreed to come with them. They said they'd help her.

"We're not going to hurry this. I want to make him sweat first. Let him know what it's like to have someone else on top for once."

"You wanna be on top?" *The other voice changed, became low and husky.* "C'mere. I'll let you be on top."

Feminine laughter shot a chill up her spine, and she backed away from the door.

She'd been fooled. They weren't doing this for her as they'd said. They wanted money. They were using her. They'd lied!

Did all adults lie?

Without thinking it out, she slid into her jeans, grabbed her high-tops and backpack. Ignoring the grunts and whispers from the other room, she tiptoed to the door, boldly shot her hand out, slipped her fingers around the knob and turned.

Nothing happened.

Oh, God . . . locked in.

Her pulse thrummed, and her heart smashed against her ribs. She flitted to the open window and peered out desperately, even knowing what she would see: a three-story drop to the ground. She'd kill herself if she tried that.

Trapped! A prisoner!

She backed into a corner. Sank to the floor. Hugged her backpack and her high-tops to her chest.

Never in her wildest imaginings had she considered this. What now? What if her father was so angry he wouldn't pay to get her back? What would they do to her then?

She couldn't panic. She had to keep her head. Hard to do when all she wanted was to cry. That and have her father holding her in his arms, telling her everything would be all right. He would forgive her if she apologized, wouldn't he? If she told him she would never run away again?

Please, Dad, please . . .

Brushing her fingers nervously across the charms, she knew she had to get to him. But how? They wouldn't let her go back, not if they wanted money for her.

The tears flowed down her cheeks. A lump stuck in her throat. She'd never been so afraid. Not even when the guy who'd given her a lift as far as Evanston had tried to maul her. Not even when she'd spent the rest of the night hiding beneath some bushes on the Northwestern campus.

Suddenly, it occurred to her that they didn't know she knew.

That was definitely to her advantage, she decided.

She slashed at her tears, swallowed the lump.

She would have to pretend. Not let them suspect a thing. She'd gotten the lead in her class play last year, and everyone had agreed she had talent. Even Dad had said she was quite a little actress. She could do it. Pretend nothing was wrong until she figured out an escape.

She would wait for her opportunity, and then she would be out of this dump so fast they wouldn't know what happened.

Only... what then?

HER CRY JOLTED TYLER up off the sofa in a single lunge. He got to the door even as she unlocked it and threw it open. He'd left only a single low light burning, and that across the unfamiliar room, but he could see well enough to know her face was pale, her eyes glazed.

Spooked, he asked, "What?"

"She's in real trouble," Keelin choked out, fisting his shirtfront. "She heard them... tried to get away. But the door was locked. And the window..."

"Heard who?"

"I don't know. A man and a woman. I didn't see." Her gaze turned inward. "Scared. So scared. Walked right into it . . ."

Realizing Keelin was speaking as if *she* were the one in trouble rather than his daughter, he gave her a sharp shake to snap her back. "Scared of what?" he demanded, his voice gruff. "What did you hear them say?"

She gasped and her eyes cleared. Her long, dark lashes fluttered over her pale cheeks. She was breathing hard, as if she'd been running. Her gaze met his, and he realized she was terrified. Her body trembled under his hands.

"What were they talking about?" he asked again, more gently this time.

"Something about a ransom note."

Tyler's heart skipped a beat. A parent's worst nightmare. His child had been kidnapped.

Chapter Four

Keelin swam up out of her dreamlike state to find herself pressed against Tyler's chest. He was holding her fast, and she was clinging to him as if it were the most natural act in the world. She vaguely reasoned that she should be uncomfortable, should push herself away to regain some distance and a perspective on the situation. This man didn't even trust her, for heaven's sake.

But the last thing she desired was to put any distance between them, she realized. His body heat was comforting... distracting....

Unexpected emotions warred through her. Forgetting his distrust, she concentrated on him. On the man in pain. She wished she could will the misery from him, absorb it herself—unreasonably, perhaps, given his antipathy toward her—or at the very least render impotent the anguish he was suffering.

She couldn't help herself. Following her natural instincts, she slid her arms around his neck and comforted him as best she could. He shuddered against her.

"It'll be all right," she whispered, only hoping she was uttering the truth.

"Keelin, I have to get her back."

"I know. I know."

"Whatever I have to do." His mouth pressed into her hair. "Anything." Whispered against her temple. "I'll do anything to get my daughter back." Trailed across her cheek. "Give them anything they want!"

Eyes stinging, heart churning with feelings she didn't understand, she turned her face up to his, felt his breath brush her skin. "I believe you."

Threading her fingers through the thickness of his dark hair, she was startled by her own boldness. For a moment, their gazes caught, and she responded to the torment she read in his eyes. Torment that came at least partly from guilt, she thought, even as her body quickened to his.

How could this be? How could her blood rush with such longing now? At such a desperate time when personal want should not matter?

"I knew Cheryl didn't really mean to run away from me," he whispered, sounding as if he were trying to deny the guilt she sensed in him, smoothing her hair so that she pressed a cheek into his hand. "Not seriously. She would have come home by now if she weren't being held prisoner."

Keelin shook her head. "Cheryl *did* run, Tyler. And she trusted whoever is now holding her prisoner to protect her. *From you.* Don't waste time fooling yourself, please." Though his expression darkened and he put her from him, gripping her shoulders hard, she didn't stop. "You need to concentrate on whoever might have pretended they wanted to help Cheryl. Maybe if you can figure out who has a motive—"

"A motive? The bastards want money, plain and simple." His gaze changed, as if he remembered sus-

pecting that's what *she* wanted of him. He suddenly let
her go and stepped back. "The greedy people in this
world are willing to do anything to get money."

Realizing he included her in that sweeping condemn-
nation, Keelin took a deep breath and tried to will
away the yearning to feel his arms around her again,
tried to harden herself against Tyler so that he couldn't
hurt her more. She couldn't do it. God help her, she
felt something for the man. And him a near-stranger.

Trying to derail her emotions, she choked out,
"Greed is only a part of it. There's more." She concentrated, tried to remember exactly what she'd heard.
"One of them said something about wanting you to
sweat, to know what it's like for someone else to be on
top."

He pulled a face. "You're saying someone is using
my daughter—a child—to punish me?"

She swallowed hard. "I believe so."

"Dear God, what have I done that's so terrible that
He would let my child suffer for it?"

An uneasy Keelin wondered the same thing.

HALFWAY THROUGH the morning, Brock was pacing
in Tyler's office. This waiting put his nerves on edge
and twisted his gut into a fancy knot. Pam had told
him the moment Ty called in. Supposedly, he was on
his way and would arrive any minute. Brock checked
his Rolex. Eighteen minutes ago now. It was out of
character—Ty's being so late. But the past few days
had been a crap shoot in general—nothing going as it
was supposed to.

He stared out the window at Lincoln Park. So many
people with no worries. Going about their pleasure as

if it was any other day. Well, it wasn't. Today was D day, and Ty had better agree to his proposal.

"Any mail?" came the deep voice from the outer office.

Brock whipped around and stared at the half-open door. He'd thought he was psyched, but Ty had somehow sneaked up on him, made him feel as if he was at the disadvantage. Sweat gathered on his forehead, along his neck, under his suit. He wasn't good at confrontation, especially not with someone as tough as his business partner. Brock knew that very quality had spelled their success...but had also caused his own discontent.

"I think the mailman was here a few minutes ago," Alma, whom Ty had hired after her husband's desertion, was saying. "Sara is probably still sorting the mail. Should be up anytime now."

"Let me know as soon as you get it, then." Ty's voice drew closer.

"Waiting for something in particular, Mr. Leighton?" the motherly receptionist called after him.

"Just let me know." Ty's voice was louder now.

In command as usual, Ty took ownership of his office the moment he walked in the door. He didn't look like a man who was suffering, Brock mused from his position at the window. Not at all like a father who feared he might have lost his only child for good.

Then Ty noticed him and frowned. "Brock. What are you doing in here?" He set his briefcase on his desk.

"Waiting to continue the discussion that got interrupted yesterday."

"I asked you to give me time."

"Time isn't going to fix things." Though guilt sneaked along his nerves, he wasn't going to back down now.

Ty sat, stared at him pensively. "I thought we were friends."

"We were. Hell, we are. I feel for you. You know I do. But this is business."

Brock wanted more than a partnership in which he faded into the woodwork. An opportunity had come up, one too good to let slip through his fingers, or he wouldn't be so fixed on leaving now. If Ty got a whiff of his plans...

"Right at this moment, I'm having trouble believing you consider us friends."

"Let's say both the friendship and the partnership are strained. Maybe the first can be recovered if the second is dissolved amicably."

"A friend would put this on the back burner until we get Cheryl home."

"Which could be never."

A thick silence followed, and he would swear that Ty paled. He went stiff as a corpse. Cold. His light blue eyes reminded Brock of shards of ice. He shifted uncomfortably under their glare. He'd seen that particular look before, but never aimed at him. He didn't relish being the recipient of the other man's ill will.

"Don't ever intimate such a thing again," Ty warned him in a low, menacing voice. "I'll bring my daughter home, and in one piece. You can bet your half of the business on that."

"I'm not betting my half of the business on anything. I just want to pack it up and leave." Despite his growing discomfort, he pushed forward. "I want half of everything. Split right down the middle. Clients, contacts, assets. Everything."

"I promise you, we'll talk about it. When I'm ready."

When *he* was ready. Wasn't that just like Ty. Decisions were always his call, Brock fumed, frustration getting the best of him. Without another word, he stormed out of the office.

Coming up the stairs, mail in hand, Pam gave him an intense, inquiring look. Not wanting her to guess what had gone on in there—how, once more, Ty had taken the upper hand—he turned his face away and escaped into his own office. The one with the view of congested Clark Street rather than the tranquil park.

His insides felt as tangled as the traffic tie-up at the intersection, but he was determined for once to get what he wanted. Cheryl really was Tyler's weak spot, and Brock knew it. He loved the kid, he really did, and he didn't want to have to use her disappearance as leverage.

But if it came to that...

For once in his life, he wasn't going to back off because something was too tough.

"Mail call." Pamela brought in half an armload and set it on Tyler's desk. "Alma said you were anxious for something or other this morning."

Tyler was already flipping through the letter-sized envelopes when he grunted, "Thanks."

He hadn't thought to disbelieve Keelin about the ransom note when she'd seemed as shaken as him. At first, he'd clung to her with trust and something more, something that cut deeper despite his worry over his daughter . . . and then . . . suspicion had reared its ugly head.

Now he didn't know what to think. How could he be certain his feeling closer to Keelin hadn't been part of her master scheme to take him in?

She'd made moves on him—throwing her arms around his neck, touching his face in that gentle way that made his heart thunder in his chest. He'd wanted to touch her and kiss her and do more than just hold her. And this while his only thought should have been of his daughter, he remembered, disgusted with himself. Keelin making him think *he* was to blame—that some enemy *he'd* made was using Cheryl to get even— could have been no more than a stroke of genius on her part. A smoke screen so that he would forget he didn't trust her. That he'd vowed never to be fooled again.

He automatically discarded any letters with a familiar return address. Two were from people he didn't know. A third had no return address at all. His fingers tightened on the ordinary white envelope that could have been purchased at any drugstore.

"Are you okay?"

Tyler glanced up at his assistant, her gaze sympathetic, but he couldn't answer. No, he wasn't okay. He wouldn't be okay until he held Cheryl in his arms. He tore open the envelope and pulled out the paper.

This was it.

No originality here. Block letters cut from magazines and newspapers glared out at him: *Don't involve the police further if you value your daughter's life. I'll be in touch.*

For a moment, he forgot to breathe. Pressure built inside him until he was ready to explode.

"Tyler?"

He looked at Pamela, at her dark eyes reflecting his own anguish. He handed her the warning missive. She blanched when she read it.

"Oh, God. What are you going to do?"

"Whatever the bastard who sent that says."

Inspecting the envelope as if he could read the sender's true intentions from it, he suddenly realized that though it had been stamped, there was no postmark. "This never went through the U.S. mail." He showed Pamela.

"You think someone slipped it into the pile when it was first delivered?"

"How else?"

"We had at least a dozen strangers wandering around downstairs this morning," his assistant admitted. "I suppose any one of them could have done it."

Or someone who was not a stranger at all, Tyler mused. *Keelin?* Definitely someone who knew him. He still couldn't get over the idea of Cheryl's going off with someone she trusted more than him....

"What about George Smialek?" Pamela suggested. "Maybe he's crazy enough to do something like this."

"He's suing me."

"But a suit isn't personal."

"You have a point." Though Cheryl didn't know the man.

"So, aren't you going to call the police?"

"No. The sender threatened to kill Cheryl if I did."

"You could give them what they want, and they could kill her anyway."

As if he hadn't thought of that.

"Pamela, I don't want you telling anyone about this."

He had to find his daughter before it came to a life-or-death situation, Tyler thought. Keelin was the key. Though he prayed she was on the up-and-up, she could be part of the scam.

One way or the other, he feared he would be forced to put his daughter's fate in Keelin McKenna's hands.

SKELLY LIVED in a posh brick-and-stone row house on Lincoln Avenue, a diagonal street cutting across Chicago's north side. The triangular development, with entrances at each of the three corners, emulated a London neighborhood. All the row houses looked over inner streets and small snatches of green. Living quarters stacked up two stories over the street-level garages.

"Quite a place you have here," Keelin said, wandering around the generously apportioned living and dining areas. She wondered if her cousin was in love with black-lacquered furniture, or if the same interior designer who'd decorated his office had had a free hand in his home, as well.

As she stood over him, Skelly frowned. "You look tired."

"Sleep seems a bit elusive these days."

"Another dream?"

She nodded. "Cheryl Leighton's in trouble." She tried not to dwell on the complex emotions she had for the girl's father, all of which troubled *her*. "She trusted the wrong people. They're going to want money to give her back."

"I'm sorry." He took a folder from his briefcase and indicated she should sit on the couch opposite him. "Especially sorry that you feel responsible for this girl. Tyler Leighton is the type of man a woman should avoid."

Skelly spread the contents across the coffee table. Keelin sat and looked over copies of newspaper articles. Actually, they were society columns, most of which were accompanied by photographs of Tyler with some woman on his arm. Rather, all different women.

And one she recognized.

"Over the years, Leighton's been seen with a number of socialites, each for a limited period of time," Skelly told her. "He's never been seriously involved with any of them as far as I know. Never lets them get too close. The latest of his conquests was Vivian Claiborne."

"We've met, so to speak." Pushing away the memory of being held in Tyler's arms, she said, "Skelly, if you're afraid Tyler will turn my head—"

"I'm afraid for your safety. He moved from Indiana—when his daughter was about two years old—after his wife died, supposedly in a car accident. Only, I couldn't get a bead on the particulars. No tragic story in any Indianapolis newspaper. No obituary. If you ask me, Helen Leighton must have died under some mysterious circumstances...."

"You're not saying you think he killed her and buried her in the backyard, are you?"

"I'm saying that it's possible. I've got a research assistant working on some other thoughts."

Remembering her caution around Tyler, having recognized his dark side, she shifted uncomfortably. Tyler a murderer? Surely not. Surely she would sense it if he were truly dangerous.

But why should she? Though she might be able to see through another's eyes, that was as far as her so-called psychic gift went. She couldn't see into another person's soul, couldn't read anyone's mind. She had to rely on her natural instincts—the same instincts that everyone possessed—to judge character.

Besides, Keelin reminded herself, Skelly sensationalized stories for a living. Maybe he was digging for a story where there was none.

She shook her head. "No, it's too bizarre."

"The strange disappearance of the first Mrs. Leighton *is* bizarre," Skelly agreed, "and that's why I want you to be careful. I don't want to chance losing my new cousin before I even get to know what makes her tick."

"You mean afterward would be all right?" she asked with a straight face.

Skelly seemed startled for a moment. Then, when he realized she was joking, he grinned. "Aileen's going to love your sense of humor. And speaking of my sister, we ought to get a move on or she might be unavailable. I don't have a clue to her bookings for today."

Keelin already knew his half sister was a massage therapist and that she'd been enthusiastic at the prospect of meeting her cousin from Ireland.

"Then we had best hurry." She indicated the copies. "Can I keep these?"

"Consider them yours."

She stuffed the papers back into the folder and took it along. She'd have the time to look them over more carefully later in her hotel.

Taking Skelly's car, they drove north up Lincoln Avenue to Aileen's place of work.

"Natural Is... is an alternate-life-style business owned by a local health-food guru," Skelly said. "It promotes a more natural way of life—from organic foods to homeopathic medicines to healing hands. There's a combination shop-café and a health clinic. Aileen is the massage therapist."

"How peculiar and grand that I share a similar interest with a cousin who was born thousands of miles from me," Keelin said with wonder.

Natural Is... was located in a double storefront in an area that Skelly told her was still recovering from an economic fallout. Two major department stores had gone out of business with most of the smaller shops following. But eventually, new businesses had moved in, loft condominiums had been created and the neighborhood had received a face-lift in general.

Keelin especially appreciated the old building facades that had been cleaned up and restored. And she felt comfortable entering Natural Is.... The reception area of the clinic was anything but sterile. Purple walls. Oriental carpets underfoot. An eclectic mix of secondhand furniture, some of it painted bright colors, scattered about. A mobile of the universe glittering in one corner. And plants peeking out from every nook and cranny. Lots and lots of plants.

And her cousin Aileen was equally colorful, wreathed in a brilliant fuchsia-turquoise-and-jade-print cocoon jacket that shimmered as she threw her arms around Keelin.

"My schedule is clear for the rest of the hour," Aileen said before Skelly could make more formal introductions. "Let's go next door to the café."

Half brother and sister had the same blue eyes, and Keelin could see a resemblance in the cheekbones and jawline. But where Skelly had black hair, Aileen was blond, her extraordinary fairness no doubt inherited from her mother, LaVerne.

Keelin knew that Skelly's mother, Faye O'Reilly—her own father's first love and the reason for the division between him and Raymond—had died shortly after Skelly's birth. Raymond had quickly remarried, but his union with LaVerne Gordon had ended in divorce. Gran had once mentioned Raymond also had a child out of wedlock, but Keelin hadn't found any letters or cards from Skelly and Aileen's half brother, Donovan, in Moira's box of cherished memories.

The café took up the front third of the other half of Natural Is.... Keelin barely got a glimpse of the displays of books, nutritional supplements and more eye-catching treasures in the store before they settled at a table overlooking the busy street. Keelin and Aileen ordered herbal teas, while Skelly stuck to a hearty coffee.

They exchanged details about their lives while waiting for their order. Once they were served, Skelly got down to business.

"It's up to you to convince Dad to make this trip back to Ireland, Aileen."

"I can try."

"She can wind him around her little finger," he assured Keelin.

Aileen shrugged modestly. "Plus, we have the advantage because Dad never did get over not seeing his mother again before she passed on last year. I can probably use a little guilt . . . uh, not that I think your father is going to die or anything," she hurriedly added.

"Use whatever ammunition you have to—right, Keelin?"

His statement reminding her of what Skelly did for a living, Keelin squirmed. "Within reason," she agreed, disliking the idea of being underhanded.

For wasn't that what Tyler thought of *her?* That she would do anything, fabricate anything, to get to his money?

She hated that Tyler Leighton could get to her even when he wasn't in her presence, when she was trying to concentrate on family, on her original mission. She hated that Tyler thought she might be a charlatan when all she wanted was to help him and his daughter.

And yourself, an inner voice reminded her.

"Dad's planning on taking the Friday-night red-eye in from Washington," Aileen was saying. "Maybe I'll surprise him—meet him at the airport."

"Get him in a weakened condition." Skelly grinned. "You'll have him agreeing before he knows what hit him."

Keelin shifted uncomfortably. It wasn't that she didn't like Skelly—she just wasn't certain that she approved of him. Or rather, of his methods.

"If he puts up a fuss," Aileen said, "I'll tell him *we're* going, with or without him."

"Will you really come?" Keelin asked.

"I've always wanted to see Ireland."

Skelly added, "I might be able to find an angle for a story. A tax write-off."

As long as the story was not about the McKennas, please God, Keelin thought.

"What about Donovan? Is he likely to agree?"

Sister and brother exchanged looks.

"Who knows what Donovan's likely to do?" Aileen said, tearing her gaze from Skelly to Keelin. "I'll tell you, it's doubtful, considering he doesn't even think of himself as one of us."

"Who even knows where Donovan is or what he's been up to for the past dozen years?" Skelly muttered less amiably, arousing Keelin's curiosity.

But having the distinct impression that Skelly would rather not talk about their mysterious half brother, she asked, "What about Aunt Rose? Do you think *she's* open to a reunion?"

"Mmm, I don't know." Skelly sprawled back in his chair. "She has the biggest reason to stay away, doesn't she, considering she was told never to darken a McKenna doorstep again."

Harsh words and hardly believable as coming from her father's lips, but Keelin knew them to be true. For centuries, "the troubles" in Éire had pitted Catholic against Protestant. When Rose had fallen in love with a man who was both Protestant and American, her brothers forbade her to see him. When she defied them, saying she would marry Charlie and go off to America with him, they felt she betrayed not only their country, but them personally. And when they had disowned her, an angry Rose cursed her brothers, wishing them the same luck in love that they wished for her.

Not long after, the brothers had bitterly fought over Faye, and Raymond won her heart. They, too, had come to America, and her uncle built a new life. Now a U.S. congressman from Chicago, he had never looked back. After Faye's death, Raymond had never found a lasting relationship with another woman.

The only triplet to remain in Éire, her own father had settled for a young girl about whom he'd had no romantic notions. And while he'd learned to love Delia in his own way, Keelin had always sensed something missing in her parents' relationship.

She could only hope that Rose had fared better with her beloved Charlie.

What she knew of the story, Keelin had gleaned directly from her grandmother. The triplets had broken Moira's heart, and thus she had created what Keelin thought of as the McKenna legacy, wishing for her grandchildren the personal happiness denied her own offspring because of their selfishness and intolerance. And for all their sakes, Keelin hoped the legacy held all the power of Moira McKenna's love.

"Maybe the best way to get to Rose would be through cousin Kate," Aileen mused, bringing Keelin back to the present.

"Kate's the veterinarian in South Dakota," Keelin recounted. "You've actually met her?"

"Years ago, when she was attending a professional conference in Chicago, she looked us up," Skelly explained.

"We're not close," Aileen added, "but we're friendly. We write a couple of times a year and call at the holidays. I'm afraid she's our only connection to Aunt Rose."

"Then let us hope that she's as close to her mother as you are to your father."

They had little more time to plot and scheme before Aileen expressed her regrets. A client was due any moment. Hugging Keelin and extracting a promise that she wouldn't leave the city before they all had a proper dinner together, Aileen flitted back to the clinic.

And Keelin's thoughts were already flitting back to her other, more pressing concern. But what to do about it? When Tyler had left her hotel suite in the early hours of the morning, he hadn't exactly been in an expansive mood. He'd said nothing about follow-up. He'd said nothing about seeing her again that day, a fact that inordinately bothered her.

She guessed it was up to her to pursue the truth... with or without Tyler's cooperation.

As they left the café, she asked, "Skelly, would you be willing to do a bit more research for me—about Tyler Leighton?"

"Sure, cuz. I'm glad you've decided to proceed with caution. What kind of info do you want?"

"Anything you can find about his business associates."

"At L&O Realty?"

"That, too, of course. But I was thinking more on the lines of an unhappy competitor. Someone who might be holding a grudge against him."

Skelly unlocked the car door for her. "You think his daughter's kidnapping could be part of a business war?"

Let him know what it's like to have someone else on top for once...

The words from the dream echoing in her head, she nodded and slipped into the passenger seat. "Could be. Or it could be more personal. I don't want to overlook any possibility. I fear we don't have much time to find Cheryl."

Skelly started the engine and pulled the vehicle from the parking spot. For once, he didn't have much to say, merely turned on the radio to a soft-rock station that played tunes from the seventies. Keelin rested her head against the car seat and let her mind drift.

Images of Tyler floated through her head. She concentrated on his various moods. Angry. Worried. Devastated. She wanted to see a smile lighting up his handsome features, happiness radiate from him. She wanted to see his daughter safely in his arms.

Halfway to her hotel, Skelly said, "I hope you know what you're doing, getting so involved with people who don't mean anything to you."

But Tyler did mean something to her. Or at least he was beginning to, and not only because she was attracted to the man physically. Despite his cautiousness with her, she was convinced he would do anything—put himself in any danger—to rescue his child. She admired that kind of selflessness, something she hadn't had in the case of Gavin Daley. And Tyler's deep feeling for family, so like her own, touched her.

While Skelly wasn't a bad sort, Keelin suspected her cousin had never been the type to put himself out on a limb for someone else.

"We're all responsible for each other," she reminded him, echoing their grandmother's sentiments. "If you spotted a stranger on the street being attacked, wouldn't you help?"

"Sure. I'd call the police. They're trained to handle violent situations. If I stuck my nose in where it didn't belong, I'd probably mess things up."

No surprise there.

"But the authorities might be too late," she argued. "Or unwilling to believe you. There are times when, knowing someone is in trouble, you're compelled to act.''

Because not acting could haunt one for the rest of her life, as she well knew.

''You're a better person than I am,'' he said caustically. ''But that's okay. What would the world do if everyone was like me?''

Act selflessly in another's behalf, Moira's legacy had charged.

Sadly enough, Keelin couldn't see Skelly living up to their grandmother's finest dreams for them. She feared that, unless he had a change of heart, he would follow in their parents' footsteps and never find the personal happiness every human being deserved.

No sooner had Keelin set foot in the hotel lobby than she saw Tyler waiting for her. Her mouth went dry, and she noted the funny feeling in her chest. Popping out of a wing-back chair, he appeared drawn, grim, and very, very determined as he closed the gap between them to intercept her.

''We have to talk.''

Taking her elbow, he guided her to the elevators. His touch, while not rough, was unyielding.

''I'm not trying to get away from you,'' she murmured, and used her free hand to press the call button.

A flush darkening his features, he let go. ''Sorry.''

Before she could ask him what had happened, a ding signaled a set of doors opening. They entered the empty car, the doors closed and they started their ascent.

''It arrived with this morning's mail,'' Tyler said.

Her pulse quickened. "The ransom note?" Somehow, she'd imagined him receiving it at home.

"No postmark, though. Someone hand delivered it."

The way he was looking at her, she had no question as to whom he included among the suspects.

"You were with me this morning until you left for your office."

"Actually, I stopped home to change first."

"But I wouldn't know that, would I?"

"Aren't we a bit defensive? I made no accusations."

"*We* are beginning to know your expressions like the back of *our* hand."

They locked gazes in silent struggle, only releasing their hold on each other with the opening of the elevator doors.

"My floor." She led the way to her suite. Once inside the sitting room, she asked, "So what did the note say?"

Tyler ran a hand through his perfect hair, leaving a mussed lock drooping over his forehead. He looked as exhausted as she felt—and as distrustful.

"That I shouldn't involve the police any further if I value my daughter's life. And that the person would be in touch. How long before the next note comes, Keelin?"

She sat. "How would I know?"

"What? No more dreams?"

Irritated, she said, "I was busy this morning."

"With?"

"Trying to get a family reunion together." Not that she wanted to go into the problematic details.

His expression skeptical, he said, "Well, now you can come home with me."

That gave her a start. Enter the lion's den willingly? "Why should I?"

"You said you knew the others in your dreams." He paced the length of the room. "Since you never met Cheryl, you can get to know her by going through her things. And by sleeping in her bed."

"Now, wait a—"

"*You* wait!" He stopped before her. "You told me yourself time was running out. And you can only connect with Cheryl when you sleep. Maybe being among her things . . . in her bed . . . will help."

And being among Cheryl's things and sleeping in the girl's bed would force her into too close proximity to the father, Keelin thought. Even though she'd convinced herself that Skelly's insinuation about Cheryl's mother was the suspicious journalist talking, how could she know what Tyler might or might not do when crossed? He had a power about him that she couldn't deny. But violence?

"I'm not certain that's such a good idea," she said, her pulse thrumming.

"Why is that, Keelin? Afraid?"

Of him? Definitely. Though Keelin suspected what she feared most was increased intimacy with the man. She didn't want to consider the physical-danger aspect.

"Your daughter's somewhere in the city," she hedged. "Better to stay as close as possible."

"For whom?" He bent over her chair, grasping the armrests, his face practically in hers. "Cheryl or you?"

Realizing what he was suggesting, she felt her irritation increase. Her temper might have a slow fuse, but he'd been striking matches since they'd met.

"I have nothing to do with what happened to your daughter," she assured him yet again. He was so close she could feel his breath waft across her face. Her heart skipped a beat in response. "I was not even here in this country when she disappeared."

"How do I know that? This family-business thing of yours is pretty dicey, if you ask me."

Placing her hand in the middle of Tyler's chest, Keelin pushed. At first, he didn't budge. She glared at him, mentally willed him to comply. As if he read her determination, he finally let her rise.

"Speak to my cousin Skelly." Her turn to pace, to work off her growing aggravation.

"Right. The tabloid journalist. I can certainly trust him."

If she didn't jump to Skelly's defense, it was because Tyler had a point. Her cousin's methods made *her* uneasy, and Tyler didn't even know him. If only Skelly hadn't done that sensational piece on Cheryl's disappearance . . . then again, if he hadn't, she would never have identified the girl before it was too late.

"How's this for a theory?" he went on, not bothering to hide his rancor. "Your cousin wanted a good story, something that would make his career. So he recruits you to help him. He tells you to pretend to have this power so you can feed me information."

His skepticism about her gift was one thing. But his continuing distrust of her motives made Keelin lose the temper she'd been hanging on to by a thread.

"I would tell you what you could do with that theory, but my mother raised me to be a lady. If you really think that I could choose to hurt a young girl—or anyone—then you'd best search for your daughter on your own!''

"Not when you can lead me to her!"

Tyler was standing over her, threatening her with his too-close presence. Part of her was afraid. Another part was seeing-red angry.

"Get out," she said far more calmly than she was feeling. She was trembling, her stomach knotting. "Before I ring the management to have someone throw you out!"

His glare intensified, and her throat went dry. She couldn't swallow. Had she pushed him too far? Would he avenge himself in his anger?

When Tyler suddenly backed off, Keelin felt faint with relief. He crossed the room, his stride quick, and didn't look back. The door slamming shut shook not only the walls, but her insides, as well. Her legs could have been made of rubber. She felt her way down into a chair.

She'd done what she had to, she assured herself, her heart still pounding.

Only... what about Cheryl Leighton?

Fearing that allowing her temper to get the better of her had sealed the girl's fate, Keelin was sick inside.

Chapter Five

As he raced out of Keelin's hotel, Tyler's insides were tied up in knots. What the hell had gotten into him? He hadn't meant to screw things up when he'd gone back to face the woman to try to figure out her true role in his daughter's disappearance. But the longer he'd waited, the more out of kilter his thoughts had spiraled, until he'd been unable to control himself.

He had to face facts; he'd lost it. He'd opened his mouth and spewed out his worst fears at Keelin without thinking things through properly. If she were innocent—*if*—he'd put her off, perhaps for good. And if she were guilty, things might go worse for his daughter. Either way, he'd been a fool.

But what to do to make things right?

Whatever it takes, a small voice inside his head insisted.

On the way back to his office, Tyler considered his dilemma from every angle, and only one plan emerged. After giving her enough time to cool off, he'd have to seek Keelin out once more. He'd have to apologize, admit that he'd been an ass, tell her that his worry for his daughter was so great that he was having difficulty getting a proper handle on things. And then he would have to charm her.

Normally, the thought of romancing an attractive woman would be more than amenable. He was no more immune to Keelin than she seemed to be to him. At times, the chemistry between them had been palpable.

But the idea of getting closer to his daughter's kidnapper made the bile rise to his throat. And if Keelin *were* genuine and only trying to help . . . how could he live with himself then?

He'd find a way.

His daughter was the only thing that mattered, he reminded himself. *His* soul, after all, had already been damned years ago.

So he would do it, charm Keelin, make her want to please him. He didn't know whether her motives were feigned or true. If he waited to find out, it might be too late. That he might trick an innocent woman who wanted only to help him was a chance he had to take.

He'd learned to live with the unspeakable once.

The second time would be easier.

LATER, KEELIN COULD hardly concentrate on the computer screen and the article Skelly had retrieved about Tyler's recent successful bid to renovate an old theater into a multiuse arts space. Their fight had been replaying through her head ever since, had kept her from catching up on that lost sleep.

She blamed herself for letting things get out of hand. Tyler was far too emotionally distressed to act rationally. She should have sidetracked his anger rather than fueling it. Normally a congenial person who would do anything to avoid a fight, she couldn't say why she'd been so contentious.

"I found several more instances when Nate Feldman lost lucrative contracts to L&O Realty."

Skelly's voice snapped her back to the research done at her request. Now she was feeling guilty at her disapproving thoughts concerning her cousin. She'd asked for a favor, and he hadn't hesitated to come through for her, even if he had insisted a research assistant had done the work while he'd videotaped this afternoon's show. She didn't care how he'd accomplished the task; he'd responded to her need. Perhaps he wasn't as removed from responsibility toward others as he would like her to believe.

"I still cannot fathom how quickly you journalists find information," she marveled as he sat in a vacant chair and wheeled closer to her.

"Thank the computer age."

"No, thank *you.*"

Skelly seemed a bit flustered, as if he didn't know how to respond. Perhaps he wasn't used to gratitude, Keelin thought. He certainly seemed more comfortable with conflict and pessimism. An outgrowth of his career choice? she wondered. Or had he merely been born with a negative view of life?

"Anyway, Nate Feldman is definitely Leighton's chief business competitor," Skelly was saying. "Whether or not he holds a grudge at losing is another question."

"Did you find anything to link him to Cheryl?"

"Not directly, but hold on. Scoot over a bit."

Keelin did as he asked, and Skelly moved in on the computer. He sped the mouse around on its pad and his fingers over the keyboard—and the images on the computer monitor changed nearly as quickly.

A moment later, they were looking at another page of the *Chicago Tribune,* this in the "Chicagoland" section. The headline indicated a christening of a factory building converted to a minimall in the Clybourn Corridor. Keelin recognized the event from the video footage in her cousin's report two days ago. Skelly used the mouse to mark the accompanying photograph, then hit a few more keys.

After a blink, the picture exploded outward, filling the screen. Tyler shaking hands with the mayor was the focus of the photograph. Cheryl stood slightly behind her father, nearly out of the frame. And on Tyler's other side, between him and the mayor, standing some distance behind...

"Feldman?" Keelin murmured, tapping the image of the balding man.

Skelly nodded. "That's him. Odd that he showed for a celebration of a job he lost, don't you think?" He scooted his chair back and faced her. "He may not even have spoken to the girl, but he obviously knew about her."

"Surely Tyler would have realized as much. Odd that he never mentioned Feldman."

Or perhaps Tyler had been waiting for *her* to do so. Would he have considered that further proof of her perfidy? she wondered.

"Maybe it never occurred to him that a business rival would be involved," Skelly mused.

"Perhaps. Did you learn anything personal about Feldman? Anything about his character that would make him capable of using a child to punish a competitor?"

"I can give you tons of business facts and figures about the man, but without hitting the streets and interviewing people who know him, it'd be impossible to analyze his personal life."

And she couldn't ask her cousin to take the time from his work to do so. Another solution came to her. "Tyler has a private investigator trying to find Cheryl."

"Checking out Feldman might be a productive use of the man's time."

"I'll suggest as much."

If Tyler would speak to her, given the way they'd parted earlier. Hopefully, he was in his office. Whatever his reaction might be to her unexpected appearance, Keelin knew she had to brave facing him.

And this time, she would not let Tyler Leighton get under her skin and derail her from her purpose.

TYLER BROODED in his shadow-filled office. He'd spent the latter half of the afternoon calling the Hotel Clareton in an attempt to charm Keelin into forgetting his earlier accusations, but she'd up and disappeared on him.

He was so frustrated that a knock at his door made him grouse, "What is it?"

Pamela poked her head inside, her topknot bobbling. "Is it safe to enter?"

He waved her in. "How come I never tick you off?"

"Who said you don't?" His assistant raised her eyebrows but appeared as easygoing as always. "Uh, you want some light in here?" Her hand reached toward the wall switch.

"Leave it be."

He thought better in the semigloom. Or maybe it was that the light would make him face things he'd prefer to avoid at the moment.

Pamela moved closer to his desk. "I had Mr. Bryant check out Keelin McKenna as you asked me to do."

Tyler stiffened. Jeremy Bryant was the private investigator he'd hired to find his daughter. "And?"

"As far as he could tell, she's genuine. No police record on anyone using that name. He couldn't find any trace of her in this city. Then he used a personal contact—a friend of a friend of a friend, as I understand—to get to immigration records. Keelin McKenna just flew in from Ireland like she said."

A weight lifted from his chest, and he realized he'd been holding his breath. Though he'd thrown around accusations with impunity, he hadn't wanted them to be true. He'd wanted Keelin to be exactly who and what she claimed. While not the last word—a con artist could probably change identities easier than he could change the blueprints for a renovation—Bryant's research indicated that Keelin was telling the truth.

"I appreciate your help."

Pamela backed off. "Sorry I can't do more."

"That makes two of us." He checked his watch. Almost five. "Go on. Leave. Get back to your life for an evening. Let me brood in peace."

"Sure."

He didn't wait for the door to close behind her. Impatient, he picked up the telephone receiver and hit Redial, mentally following the rash of beeps that followed.

"Hotel Clareton."

"Is Miss McKenna in yet?"

"No, I'm sorry, sir," came the aggravating reply. "But if you would like to leave *another* message . . ."

Having left two already and realizing the clerk recognized his voice, Tyler felt foolish. "No message."

He slammed down the phone. For all he knew, Keelin was in and avoiding him. So what next? He crossed to the windows and stared down at the park. He was trying to come up with some options when his office door opened again.

Thinking Pamela had returned, he gruffly said, "I thought I told you to go home."

"Of the many desperate things you said to me, that was not among them."

The Irish lilt plucked at his insides, coiled around him as he turned to face Keelin. Wreathed in a flowing sunflower yellow jumper over a white T-shirt, her cloud of hair a low-flickering flame brushing her shoulders, she was a bright spot against the gloom.

They spoke as one.

"I was an ass."

"You were frantic about your daughter."

Tyler realized Keelin had come to make things right with him. She'd chosen to forgive—or at least to ignore—his accusations. Either that, or she was a very, very clever con artist. He had to consider the last option so that guilt wouldn't stop him from doing what he had to . . . to cover all bases. He couldn't screw up again.

Registering a regretful expression, he moved closer. "It seems emotions were running high on both sides earlier."

"I wish you could accept me for who I am, Tyler, but if you cannot, you cannot." Her fingers tightened on the strap of the large leather bag swung over her shoulder. "Your suspicions will not sway me from my purpose."

He couldn't be swayed, either, couldn't afford to lose sight of his plan. Despite his investigator's not finding anything remotely incriminating about her, he couldn't let down his guard around Keelin. Too much was at stake. He couldn't trust anyone or anything but himself.

He began the seduction by saying, "You have a generous heart," his tone as sincere as he could manage. He nearly believed it himself.

Her eyes widened in surprise. "I carefully considered what you said," she stated, not responding to his compliment. "About being closer to Cheryl through her things."

He was startled. "You're talking about coming home with me. You're willing?"

She nodded. "If you still wish me to."

"That would be best." He crossed the room to her. "We can stop by your hotel and—"

"No need. I brought a few things." She indicated the leather bag.

So much the better, he told himself. He could begin drawing her in immediately. Keelin's being in his territory would make his goal that much easier. So why was he having so much difficulty at working up the proper enthusiasm?

THOUGH TYLER HAD MADE an attempt at an apology, Keelin didn't fool herself into believing he trusted her. She could feel his suspicion simmering below the surface. Not that she blamed him, nor did it matter. Nothing could sway her from her course of action.

Despite her apprehension, she felt her tension dissipate as they left the city behind and entered an affluent area where the houses were mansions, some clustered together, others solitary and facing the lake. A few even had coach houses that mirrored the main quarters. She caught sight of an outdoor swimming pool on one estate, clay tennis courts on another and, as they kept driving, more and more wooded areas separating the properties.

The ravines.

A thrill shot through her as she envisioned herself—rather, Cheryl in her initial dream—stumbling down the incline, brush thrashing around her legs, the sound of turbulent waves battering the shore. Feeling as if her heart were going to burst.

Keelin's blood pulsed at an alarming rate, and she had to take a deep breath to calm herself.

"You all right?"

Tyler's tone held the right amount of concern, and yet she grew more tense. "I'll survive."

"We're almost there. Only a few more minutes."

A few minutes of curves and hills and ravines that grew deeper and denser. By the time they popped up over a knoll and turned into a driveway, Keelin had dug her nails into her seat's upholstery in anticipation.

Tyler pulled the Jaguar into the carport. Keelin didn't wait for him to open her door, but popped out and breathed in the lake-scented air. Her eyes strayed to the ravine to the south, and again she mentally replayed Cheryl's escape into the night and wondered if retracing the girl's steps along the wooded gully would be of any help.

"I'll take your bag," Tyler suddenly said, giving her a start. He was directly behind her.

"No. I have it."

She slung the leather strap over her shoulder and circled the car, making for the entrance with its high double doors. She would begin inside.

Tyler unlocked the house for her, and she entered as if in a dream. The marble floor whispering beneath her booted feet felt familiar. She recognized the free-form winged sculpture, passed by the formal living area and went straight for the smaller room off the foyer.

Tyler's office.

Standing in the doorway and gazing at the heavy mahogany desk, she felt as if she'd actually been inside, had ransacked his drawers for the money he kept for emergencies.

"You seem mesmerized."

"It's all so...odd." Her pulse danced to a strange rhythm. "I've never been here before, and yet..."

"You feel as if you have, through Cheryl." Tyler wrapped an arm around her back, his hand lightly resting on her shoulder. "I can't imagine how difficult this is for you," he said solicitously. "Maybe you'd like to sit down and catch your breath."

Not unaffected by his touch, Keelin had to fight to remember why she was there. "Her room."

In a haze, she pulled away from Tyler and turned to the staircase. She slowly climbed, hesitated halfway and purposefully tested the next step.

The wood creaked. And a chill shot up her spine.

Barely aware of Tyler's following, she continued ascending and with unerring instinct turned to her right. She kept going until she reached a room halfway down the hall. She opened the door and entered.

No doubt in her mind that this was a teenager's room. Cheryl Leighton's bedroom. A place at once both familiar and alien.

In her dream, she'd merely gotten vague impressions of the heartthrob and New Age and sports posters tacked to hot-pink walls. The futon Cheryl used as a bed lay open, a worn stuffed dog with a torn ear at its foot—the only indication that the teenager was still a child—the covers mussed as if Cheryl had just risen. A corner wall unit held a computer, sound system and television. Books, videotapes, computer programs and CDs were scattered across nearby shelves, these a brilliant purple. Keelin could see shoes and clothes strewn about the closet. The floor of the private bathroom was also a repository of discarded clothing and a pile of used towels.

"I told the cleaning woman to stay out of here." His expression grim, Tyler stood at the door as if reluctant to enter, his hands stuffed into his trouser pockets. "Stupid, but I keep thinking that nothing is changed.... I keep expecting to see Cheryl curled in bed with her headset on...or at her computer, playing a game or flying through cyberspace."

Remembering how easily Skelly had whipped along through sources of information using his computer, Keelin nevertheless eyed the electronic contraption warily. She lived several decades separated from the technology that Tyler's child took for granted. She dropped her leather bag near the futon and circled the room, touching the girl's things, almost as if she expected to *feel* her.

"Anything?" Tyler asked.

She shook her head. "I dream through another's eyes. That's the extent of my gift, as I told you.

Awake, I cannot conjure her. I agreed to come with you so I could get to know Cheryl better. Or to remember something I missed. Perhaps to find some material indication as to her intentions.''

She couldn't miss the disappointment he quickly masked as he said, ''Of course.''

Compassion made her cross to Tyler and place her hand on his arm. The physical link drew her closer to this distrusting, angry man, even as she knew keeping her distance would be a far wiser course. ''Come.'' Hooking her fingers around his arm, she drew him into the room.

He moved with her as if mesmerized, confused. As if, for a moment, he forgot what he was about. Their gazes held. He allowed her in . . . and she felt his pain with agonizing clarity. Then he blinked, as if awakening from a spell, and a subtle change came over him. She suddenly found herself shut out.

''Where shall we start?'' he asked.

For the next hour, they browsed through the items on the teeming shelves, hoping for some clue as to Cheryl's state of mind. Looking for anything that would jog Keelin's memory. Nothing. They didn't even find the address book that Keelin had hoped for. No reference to acquaintances in the city.

''She must know all her friends' telephone numbers by heart,'' Keelin murmured.

''More likely, they're programmed into her phone.''

Surrounded by Cheryl's things, they were sitting on the floor together, Keelin's legs swept behind her, Tyler's before him, his knees up, his ankles crossed. How odd that they seemed of a mind at last. They'd worked seamlessly together, and Tyler hadn't uttered one biting word since they'd begun.

Moving to the bottom shelf, Keelin chose one of several scrapbooks and began paging through photos and souvenirs that were several years old. Her eyes were tired and threatened to close on her at any moment, but she forced herself to examine each page before going on to the next.

Thinking talking would keep her awake, she said, "Tell me about your daughter."

Tyler flipped through a magazine and threw it onto a growing pile. "Cheryl's bright and passionate about life," he said, sounding every bit the proud parent. "She's trusting, big hearted and, I fear, too easily hurt. She's easy to anger... and easy to..."

"Forgive?"

"I always thought so."

But not now? What wasn't he telling her? she wondered. What had he done that his daughter was finding hard to forgive? What lies could he have told her that were so terrible that Cheryl had felt betrayed enough to run away?

Tempted to ask directly, Keelin bit back the question. Asking would only anger him. Better that she wait until he was ready to share whatever it was that was eating him up inside. Though she had no extraordinary powers beyond her mysterious dreams, she had the natural instinct that every person possessed. Perhaps she was more attuned to her intuitive side than some, for she was certain Tyler's harshness was meant to cover up his own feelings of guilt.

"Cheryl sounds a bit like Flanna," she said, going on to another scrapbook, this one older. "My sister. And my grandmother Moira, too."

She was looking at Cheryl's baby book, Keelin realized as Tyler said, "I thought *you* were like your grandmother."

His attention was on a stack of CDs, hers on the faded photographs of the infant and her parents.

"We shared some traits, yes. But I think we're all a bit like her in some way or other. Flanna has a wildness about her that was definitely Moira's."

Tyler's late wife had been stunning, curvaceous and blond, Keelin noted. And she was a natural model. She knew how to make love to the camera, and the camera, in turn, had loved her. Plus, in each photograph where they posed together, Tyler wore the besotted expression of a truly happy man.

A stab of envy made her quickly close the album, telling herself that she'd find nothing of value in these pages. She slid it to the side with the others.

"Cheryl sounds very different from you," she mused. Or at least different from what he'd become since losing his young wife. "Does she favor her mother?"

"Cheryl's nothing like her mother!" His voice was so vehement that his words sent a chill through her.

He sounded as if he hated the woman—and more than a decade after her death. And yet the love he'd had for his young wife was obvious in those photographs. Uneasy, she wished she hadn't brought up the subject.

To break the tension, she turned the conversation back to her own family. "I wish I were more like Moira."

"How so?" he asked, his words clipped.

"She was a woman who drew people and creatures alike to her. More important, she was so unafraid of who she was."

He seemed to let down his guard when he asked, "What do *you* have to fear?"

Her gift. Not knowing if she could ever live up to its expectation of her.

People.

Him.

"Sometimes . . . everything," she admitted.

His dark eyebrows slashed upward. "You could have fooled me."

Warmth crept through Keelin. Tyler almost sounded as if he admired her. A little flustered, she chose another of Cheryl's scrapbooks—this one newer than the others—and turned back the cover. A large glossy print of father and daughter stared back at her. They stood in the shelter of some trees. The facades of buildings behind them had a medieval look, as did several costumed people. A summer fair. Cheryl looked only slightly younger than she had in the news clip Skelly had shown of her. This probably had been taken the year before.

As she studied the pretty face she had never seen in person, Tyler urged, "So tell me more about this grandmother you wish you were like."

She looked up at him. "She was quite unconventional for a woman of her day. She married late. The thirty-third day after her thirty-third birthday, to be exact."

Hence, part of Moira's legacy.

"Ah, a superstitious woman."

"More to the point, the people who lived in the area were superstitious, including the young men who feared to pursue her. Some called her a witch."

"Because of the dreams?"

She nodded. "And because she had the power to heal. We had that in common also—our love of the land and of the plants that could ease suffering." Seeing the shadow sweep over his face, she quickly added, "Gran also talked to the animals, both domestic and wild, and swore she understood what they said in return."

"Most people *would* consider that a little strange," he agreed, his expression lightening, making him appear even more handsome.

Her pulse skittering strangely, she said, "And the men of the surrounding villages were timid romantically because of these things. Moira Kelly would have none of them with their weak natures. She wanted a real man, her equal."

"Since you're here, she obviously got what she wished for."

"Eventually. Seamus McKenna came to her rescue at a desperate time." Keelin remembered the tale her grandmother had repeated both with sadness and joy many times through the years. "A child Gran tried to heal died. There was no helping it, for the parents waited too long and expected a miracle. The fever took the lad. But the family blamed Moira, came after her, determined to burn the witch in her enchanted cottage."

"But Seamus stopped them."

She nodded. "A tinker by trade, he lived on the road in a caravan and made his way by fixing tools and such for people. He was repairing a drying rack in

Moira's herb shed when trouble arrived. He protected Moira with his own life and so won her heart. She, in turn, tamed a bit of the wildness in him, enough to convince him to settle down with her.''

"Sounds like a fairy tale."

"My family is from Éire, after all," she said, grinning. How good it felt to smile, to feel days of tension drain from her, if only for a short while. "A land of many wondrous tales."

"You'll have to tell me more."

He made it sound as if she would be around for an indefinite period, as if he was suddenly enjoying her company. And despite the many heated words that had passed between them, despite the distrust that still lingered like a dark shadow in the background, she found the idea of spending some peaceful time with him oddly appealing.

"Sometime, perhaps," she said softly. "But at the moment, I fear I am talked out."

Before she knew what he was about, he cupped her chin in his hand and tilted her face to his. Though he held her gently, she could feel the imprint of each finger. Her breathing nearly stopped. His pale blue eyes seemed to take in every detail of her features, and the longer he studied her, the harder her heart thudded.

And for a moment, she lost it.

Sense.

Purpose.

Everything but the need to give and take comfort.

He lowered his head a fraction, found her mouth. She opened to him, invited him in. Fiercely, he entered, and she felt as if his frustration with his powerlessness battered her. But she was stronger than she'd implied. She seized his demons and matched them with a potency of her own.

For a long, long moment, they lost themselves to each other. Male to female. Strength to softness. Determination to compassion. She had never felt so lost in a simple kiss.

A low moan shuddered through her. She pressed closer, her body flamed with wanting.... And then she came to her senses, remembered what she should be about. She broke the kiss.

When he raised his head, Tyler appeared as astonished as she, and even more flustered. But though her fingers strained against his arm, she made no immediate move away from him. Instead, she waited, her gaze twined with his, anxious to see what he would do, to hear what he would say to her, now that their alliance had taken a new twist.

Seemingly in a quandary, he sat frozen for a moment, his tension clear. He took a deep breath, then carefully backed off—a neutral move that put some distance between them without offending.

"You look exhausted," he said sympathetically.

So he was going to avoid talking about what had just happened. Too bad she couldn't ignore the feel of his mouth that lingered against hers.

"'Tis the jet lag." *And the dreams*. She couldn't remember her last full night's sleep.

"Maybe you'd like to freshen up and rest until dinner. We can continue going through Cheryl's things afterward."

A sensible suggestion. "A short rest would be grand." If truth be told, Keelin felt as if she could sleep for hours and hours. And she definitely needed time alone, away from Tyler, to regain her bearings.

A sudden thought occurred to her. She eyed him warily. "And who will be doing the cooking?"

He laughed as he rose to his feet. "Don't worry. Mrs. Hague—that's the housekeeper—cooks in big batches once or twice a week and leaves meals enough for two in the freezer. Everyone says a dog is man's best friend. I say it's the microwave oven."

He was still grinning when he held out his hand to her. She slipped her hand in his, allowing him to steady her as she got to her feet. She swayed toward him and caught herself just before they touched again.

"Hmm, maybe I should have had the room straightened," he mused.

His glance at the unmade bed sent tension humming through her. "No problem," she said, when really there was.

The growing attraction...the imaginings...the unexpected kiss.

"There are clean linens in the closet." As if realizing he was still holding on to her, he stared down at her hand for a moment before releasing it. Then he started for the door. "I'll let you know when I'm ready to put dinner in the microwave."

Keelin nodded and closed the door behind him. Touching her forehead to the wood panel, she sighed and went limp. Either she was fooling herself or Tyler was experiencing a change of heart toward her. He was treating her as if he wanted them to be friends.

Or perhaps more.

A scary thought.

Something to dream on.

Chapter Six

She died a little as she waited until the apartment grew quiet except for the game show on the TV in the living room, the announcer's voice backed by the intermittent sound of snoring.

Stemming her rising excitement, she forced herself to wait a moment longer. Until she was sure.

One of her jailers had left directly after they'd eaten, never suspecting that she knew what they were up to. Then she'd volunteered to do the dishes, had acted as if she were ever so grateful because they were keeping her safe and off the streets. She'd even gotten the first beer from the fridge.

Then she'd gone to her room to wait.

For the past hour, her ear pressed to the door, she'd listened to channel-surfing and the toilet flushing, interspersed by the refrigerator door opening and more beer tops popping.

Now she decided it was time.

Trembling inside, her stomach so knotted it ached, she grabbed her backpack and very quietly turned the door handle. Knowing it would creak if she opened it all the way, she carefully swung the panel only far enough to squeeze through. She slid into the shadows of the narrow hall and held her breath.

From her vantage point, she could see the TV and the back of the chair from which an arm dangled, fingers pointing to the half-dozen beer cans littering the floor below. Asleep. Rather, passed out.

Better for her.

Her heart thrumming with excitement, she backed up. Slowly. Silently. One high-top-shod foot behind the other. Eyes glued to what she could see of her solitary jailer. No movement from the living room except the images on the TV.

Then she was at the door.

Unlocking.

Opening.

Slipping through the crack.

The hall was dark, the landing light out. She felt her way to the stairwell. Hung on to the rail as she flew down the steps as fast as her feet would take her. On the second-floor landing, she grazed a silver-haired woman wearing wire-rimmed glasses.

"Sorry," she muttered, dancing around the elderly lady, whose arms were loaded with groceries.

"What's yer hurry?" the woman yelled after her. "Kids!"

But she was already a landing away. First floor.

Through the glass-inset door, its lock broken. Down scuzzy, chipped marble steps.

Out the front door and past three marijuana-smoking teenage boys on the front stoop.

"Hey, baby, not so fast—I got something for you," one of them called after her.

She glanced over her shoulder to see the offered joint. Three sets of glazed eyes stared at her. Three mouths trembled in smirks as if they could smell her fear. One of the boys took a step off the stoop toward her.

She ran, their laughter ringing in her ears, and utilized every bit of speed she could muster.

A few minutes later, turning off the side street onto a busier one, she headed for the crazy intersection ahead. Three streets crossing one another. She was passing an old-fashioned newsstand tucked on one of the six corners when she heard an elevated train screech to a stop. Whirling, she spotted the station. She thought to go for a train that would take her downtown. But that would only bring her back to the same dire situation she'd started in.

Then she spotted them—a couple of outdoor telephones on the angled street. She wanted to talk to her dad. Surely he would tell her what to do. Maybe even come for her.

She begged for change for a dollar at the newsstand. Then, taking her life in her hands, she crossed against the lights, weaving her way through the traffic, while horns blared and curses were hurled at her.

Only one of the phones worked. She inserted coins in the slot and dialed.

C'mon, Dad, be home . . . forgive me . . . please!

Uneasy, she eyed the foot traffic at the nearby tattoo parlor while listening to the phone ring for what seemed like an eternity. A biker couple in black leather pants and T-shirts came out, the guy admiring the tattoo on his girlfriend's breast. Suddenly, the ringing stopped.

"Hello?"

The lump in her throat was so big, she had trouble forcing out "Dad!"

"Cheryl? My God, baby, where are you?"

He sounded glad to hear her voice. Inside, a dam broke. Tears flowed from her eyes, and she choked out, "I'm sorry, Dad. Honest. I'll never do it again."

"Where are you?"

"I'm not sure. In the city somewhere."

"Look for a street sign. Ask someone. I'll come get you."

"You will? Really? You're not angry?"

He was saying, "I'm worried...not angry at you," when she felt the hand on her shoulder.

"Jeez, I'll be off in a minute!" she said impatiently.

And then the hand covered her mouth, and she knew she was in trouble. Her head went light with renewed fear. The phone flew from her hand, and the buildings around her whirled crazily as her legs folded and the pavement rushed up to meet her....

"CHERYL!" His heart pounding, his hope soured to fear, Tyler clutched the cordless phone harder, as though he could make his daughter answer. "Cheryl, baby, what happened? Please tell me you're all right!"

But all he heard was the sound of street traffic and the repeated clunk of the phone on the other end, as if it were swinging free and banging against something solid.

"Cheryl?" he said, trying one last time.

Then someone replaced the receiver in its cradle, and the line went dead.

His joy turned to renewed grief, Tyler blindly pitched the cordless phone with all his strength. The bottles in a small wine rack crashed to the kitchen floor like pins scattered by a bowling ball. One bottle broke, and a deep red pool seeped across the pale ceramic floor.

Like blood would ooze across his daughter's fair skin.

The sudden tragic image drove him crazy. Carelessly, he retrieved the broken glass, then yelped. His hand had struck a jagged edge. He was heaving the now-bloody glass into the trash when he heard the stair squeak, followed by his name.

"Tyler?" Keelin called, her voice faint and frightened. "Where are you?"

The pain of the cut momentarily forgotten, he rushed out of the kitchen as she stepped off the staircase. They met in the foyer. One look at her dazed expression and he knew.

"You were sleeping. You saw something?"

"Cheryl escaped the building where she was being held. She ran." Keelin took a big breath. "I saw busy streets. An intersection. The telephone..."

"She called me." His chest tight, he demanded, "What the hell happened?"

Keelin squeezed her eyes shut and touched her shoulder. "A hand, here."

"She told the person to wait a minute."

"Then his hand covered..." Her fingers moved over her lips.

Tyler would kill the bastard if he ever got hold of him. Suddenly, he stilled. "You said *his*. You saw him?"

Keelin's features pulled together in a frown. "I'm sorry. His grip was so strong I assumed it was a man, but then before I could turn, everything went spinning...."

Suddenly, he realized that Keelin was speaking in the first person, as if the incident had actually happened to her. She was white as a ghost, no doubt nearly as traumatized by the incident as his daughter.

Without thinking, he spread his arms and stepped forward to comfort her. She accepted the shelter he offered, flying into his embrace and clutching him like a lifeline. She was trembling, her breathing ragged. He gathered her close to him, careful not to touch her with his bloody hand. He imagined that he could feel the uneven fluttering of her heart through the wall of his chest.

Before, when she'd told him about the dream-visions, he'd only half believed her. How could he deny her gift any longer when he'd been part-witness to what she'd experienced? He'd been on the line with Cheryl when Keelin had tuned in. Her explanation of what she'd seen fit exactly with his own perception of what had happened to his daughter. Against all reason, he had to believe in a phenomenon that had no logical explanation.

"It's going to be all right." As if in a trance, he ran his good hand soothingly through Keelin's loose, lush hair and down her supple spine. Touching her so intimately had a very real and immediate effect on him, one he didn't want to acknowledge. "We're going to make sure it's all right. We'll find Cheryl. Together."

When Keelin gazed up at him, her eyes were shiny. "Truly?" she asked.

"I promise."

A smile trembled on her lips even as she blinked, and a few tears freed themselves from her thick, dark lashes. He couldn't help himself. He kissed the trail on her cheek. His lips instantly salty, he ran his tongue over them, vaguely wondering what he was doing.

How was it that he was getting caught up in the very woman he'd vowed to entice in return for his daughter's safety?

As if she could read his mind, Keelin vowed, "I would do anything to bring Cheryl home to you."

Her warm breath fluttered against his face. He couldn't help but believe her.

Suddenly, Keelin noticed the blood dripping from his hand. Eyes wide, she demanded, "What happened?"

"I just nicked myself on some broken glass."

"That's more than a nick. Let me."

She took his wrist and raised his hand so she could see the wound. Over his murmured objections, she pulled him into the kitchen and to the sink. Keeping pressure below the cut, she washed it out with an antiseptic liquid soap and checked it for any stray pieces of broken glass.

Then she placed his free hand at a pressure point below the cut and ordered, "Keep your hand up, the wound above your heart, and hold that pressure steady. I'll get my first-aid kit."

Keelin raced upstairs, pulled the soft-sided kit from her leather bag and ran back to the kitchen. She set it on the counter and removed a few items.

"What's that?" Tyler asked suspiciously.

"Wicked remedies that will render you powerless."

She delivered the answer with a straight face and would have been amused at Tyler's uneasy reaction if he weren't hurt. Soaking a swab in witch hazel, she cleaned the cut. Minus the still-oozing blood, it didn't look so bad.

"Witch hazel helps stop the bleeding," she said, "but keep the hand upright." She opened a small jar. "And pot-marigold cream is an antiseptic."

Smoothing the cream over his wound shouldn't have been a sensual experience, but touching him made her heart beat a bit faster anyway. She felt his gaze on her and she looked straight into his eyes. Something inside her responded.

Confused, she turned away and put her potions back in their nest, taking longer than necessary to regain her balance.

"A small bandage and we're done," she pronounced.

This time she was careful as to how she touched him when she applied the strip. She avoided anything but the most impersonal contact.

"Good as new," he said. "It doesn't even hurt. Much."

"Remind me to apply more pot-marigold cream later."

"You made these wicked potions yourself?"

She nodded. "As I did the rest of my herbal first aids."

"And you carry these everywhere?"

Thinking he sounded a tad too amused, she raised her eyebrows. "Would a doctor travel without his bag?"

"Probably not." Seeming embarrassed, he moved away and quickly unrolled some paper towels straight into the mess he'd made. "Do you think you can recognize the place in the dream?"

"The building they're keeping her in?" She thought a moment but realized Cheryl hadn't focused on anything but the teenagers leering at her. "No."

Tyler threw the used towels in a waste container and fetched some loose bottles, setting them on the counter. "What about the area she called from?"

"Perhaps." Images replayed in her mind's eye. "Yes, I think so."

"Describe it to me."

"A very busy place. Streets crowded with cars and lorries. And a commuter train on tracks raised above the street."

"An el. She was near an elevated train! That eliminates most of the city," he said, excitement nearly bursting from him as he recovered the cordless phone and checked it, then threw it on the counter. "What else?"

"Shops. Places to eat."

"A commercial district."

"And the telephones—they were outside, on the sidewalk."

"I figured. The sound of traffic was pretty clear." He frowned. "Can you remember the name of any particular restaurant or store?"

Some vague memory nagged at her, but she shook her head. "Cheryl was so panicked, I don't think she noticed many details."

"At least we have a start in our search for her," he said, sounding encouraged. "We can drive around checking out neighborhoods near each of the elevated lines until you recognize some landmark. We don't have much time, a couple of hours until dark—"

They were racing for the door when the sound of a car engine directly outside the house made Tyler curse.

"Now, who can that be?"

"The authorities?" she suggested as he crossed the foyer ahead of her. "Perhaps they found Cheryl!"

When he opened the door, however, a woman stood on the other side. All Keelin saw was long, sleek, light brown hair haloed with lighter streaks so dramatic that they looked as if an artist had brushed them on.

"Tyler. You're certainly not looking the worse for wear," the stranger said, her voice low and throaty.

"Helen!" He spit the name as if he hated it. "What the hell are you doing here?"

"Aren't you going to invite me in?"

"Damn you—"

"Then I'll invite myself."

The woman pushed past Tyler, and Keelin saw that she was fashionably dressed in a gray silk shorts suit, the jacket topping a halter the same brilliant red as her slim belt, chunky heels and bag. She stopped when they came face-to-face. They were of an age, yet this woman was everything she was not, Keelin realized. Stunningly beautiful. The kind of body that tempted a man beyond endurance. Stylish. Most of all, confident.

Painted red lips quivered into a smile as the woman gave her a once-over in return. "You must be Tyler's newest playmate," she purred, holding out her hand. "I'm his wife, Helen Dunn Leighton."

HELEN GOT great satisfaction at the expression of disbelief mingled with horror that she'd inspired in the mouse of a woman who didn't seem to notice the offered hand. Helen let it drop. Really. She'd thought Tyler had better taste, cultivating the crème de la crème of society babes. This one didn't even know how to dress, for heaven's sake. She looked like a throwback to the seventies, with that shapeless rag she was wearing. What a pity if this was the best Tyler could attract these days.

"Helen is no longer my wife," Tyler assured the other woman in a low voice before grabbing *her* arm and spinning her around. "And she's just leaving."

Fury filling her, Helen ripped her arm free. "You're not getting rid of me so easy this time!"

Tyler stuck his face in hers. "You're not staying."

He enunciated each word as if she couldn't understand English. Her pulse might be thundering, but she wasn't really afraid of him. Not anymore. Not when she was holding the winning hand for once.

Sweetly, she countered, "Cheryl's home?"

"No."

"Then I'm not going anywhere." She waltzed into the living room, calculated the worth of the classic furnishings and the artwork. "Not when my daughter is missing."

Tyler dogged her. "You care more about your nails than you do about Cheryl."

She whirled on him. "Don't tell *me* what I care about!" The resentment at his using Cheryl against her was as fresh as if it had happened yesterday. "I've had enough of your righteousness to last me a lifetime!"

She could see he was holding on to his restraint by a bare thread when he said, "We'll go into it at another time, Helen. We were just about to leave."

"A date? How sweet. And with Cheryl somewhere out there on the streets."

"We're going to try to find her."

This from the woman. The mouse had an accent. Irish?

Helen raised her eyebrows questioningly. "And how do you plan to find *my daughter?*"

"Our business is none of yours," Tyler stated.

That ticked her off good. She'd like to know his every move. She'd like him answering to her. But she would get what she wanted soon enough. He was vulnerable. She could see beyond the belligerent expression. He was hurting, hurting good if not as much as he deserved to.

"Then go." She strolled to a couch and sat, making certain Tyler got a good view of her legs. He'd always had a weakness for her legs. "I'll find everything I need."

His eyes were shards of ice when he flicked them from her legs to her face. "What the hell do you think you're doing, Helen?"

"What do you expect me to do when my daughter is missing, Tyler?" she demanded.

"Stay out of Cheryl's life as you've always done."

"As you forced me to do!"

"As you happily took money to do," he reminded her. "I'll let you know what's going on when I learn something concrete. Where are you staying?"

"This place must have a few extra bedrooms not in use."

"You're not staying here."

"Damn if I'm not."

"Don't make me use force."

Helen glared at him and narrowed her gaze. "Don't make *me.*"

"What's that supposed to mean?"

She studied her acrylic nails that his money paid for and frowned at a chip in the bright red polish. "You wouldn't want me spilling everything to the press, now, would you?''

Triumph filled her when Tyler glowered. He appeared as if he wanted to strangle her. She recognized the expression. And she remembered the feel of his hands on her throat, his thumbs at her windpipe.

Despite her hatred for him, something inside her stirred. Her nipples hardened, straining against the silk of her halter top. Perversely, she figured a tumble with Tyler now would be far more exciting than when he'd been willing to cater to her every whim.

He was stronger.

But so was she.

She gave the mouse a pointed look. ''So you're Tyler's latest bimbo.''

''Leave her out of this.''

Helen ignored the threat in his tone. ''He won't marry you. He wouldn't admit to having been married to me if it weren't for Cheryl.''

''You have that one right.''

''*Bimbo* must be one of your quaint American expressions,'' the other woman said. ''A term *you* seem to be quite familiar with.''

Helen gaped. The mouse was smart, maybe even had claws. She suddenly grew uneasy under the soft gray eyes that seemed to peel away her skin. The feeling made her itch.

''Just get on with whatever you have to do,'' she told them, imperiously waving her hand. ''I'll be waiting breathlessly for some news, so do call if you learn anything about Cheryl.''

When Tyler didn't immediately move, the Irishwoman put a hand on his arm. ''You said we did not have much time.''

The virulence drained out of him when he gazed at her. Helen clenched her jaw. She recognized *that* look, as well. He'd aimed it at *her* often enough during their short courtship and marriage.

"You're right, Keelin." Then to Helen, Tyler said, "I'd prefer you were gone when we return. But if anything is missing ..."

How dare he intimate that she was a thief!

She glared daggers at his back as he escorted that Keelin bitch out of the house. She'd never taken anything from him but what she had coming.

He, on the other hand, hadn't been nearly so fair.

Now it was his turn to suffer.

As TYLER DROVE like a madman, Keelin tried to assimilate the scene they'd just left. He was equally silent, strained. His fingers curled around the wheel as if choking it. She couldn't guess at his dark thoughts.

"Cheryl did say she was in the city somewhere." Tyler's words were stiff. "So although elevated trains run into the North Shore, I'm going to start in Rogers Park at the city boundary."

Keelin waited until they'd traversed a few suburbs, until Tyler's muscles seemed to relax a bit, before she broached the subject that lay between them.

"I was under the distinct impression that your daughter's mother was dead," she observed.

Even Skelly had said so... though he hadn't been able to find the evidence in print, making him think that Tyler had done something untoward. At least Tyler hadn't buried the body in the backyard.

"Too bad Helen's *not* out of the way for good," he muttered, his malice putting a lump square in Keelin's throat until he added, "Not that I really wish her dead. I am glad that we are well and truly divorced, however. I don't know where she gets off telling you she's my wife."

For effect, Keelin was certain.

"Divorce is common in the United States." If against the church in her own Catholic country. "Why say a woman is dead if she isn't?"

"Because I wanted her dead to my daughter!"

Though taken aback at his vehemence, she asked, "Isn't that a bit . . . cruel?"

"Would it be kinder to tell Cheryl that her mother was so avaricious she chose money over her own daughter?"

"You're the one who paid Helen to give up her child, are you not?"

"Big-time," he said, obviously missing her irony. "And I'm still paying. It was a forever kind of deal."

"I don't understand."

"I don't expect you to."

And he obviously wasn't about to try to explain.

What had she assumed? That one kiss would change him? Make him more open to her? Trusting?

She tried to let it go, but his cruelty amazed her. Separating a mother and her child was unnatural. How could he? Even if Helen was one of the most unpleasant women she'd ever met, she was still Cheryl's mother. Such rancor on Tyler's part. Why? Because his wife couldn't live with him anymore?

She left her questions unasked and concentrated instead on the real victim. Cheryl. She had to think of the daughter, for her current thoughts on the father were beyond bearing. And this so soon after they'd taken a step closer to each other . . . close enough to make her imagination spin.

They passed Northwestern University, and then the Jaguar nosed along a stretch with the lake on one side, a cemetery on the other, reminding Keelin of Tyler's lie.

"We're just about there." A moment later, he made a turn onto another street. "See—the elevated structure ahead. Tell me if anything looks familiar."

She gave the street a thorough scanning as they passed under the honeycomb of steel beams. "Nothing."

Tyler turned the corner and, staying within sight of the elevated tracks, wove back and forth along several main arteries with rapid-transit stations. She kept watch, hoping she would recognize some small detail.

"I believe we're in the wrong neighborhood," she told him. "This simply has a different feel. A bit newer, perhaps."

"Then we'll move on." He crossed under the steel structure where it turned. "I'm planning on following this line all the way, until it goes underground. Then we'll check the other rapid-transit lines if we must."

"How many are there?"

"On the north side, both the Ravenswood and the Jefferson Park lines run above ground for quite a stretch."

"And there are more in other parts of the city?"

"A couple. The elevated line loops around the financial-commercial heart of the city, though there's no real neighborhood anywhere nearby. Another elevated track travels west. I think the southbound rapid-transit lines run strictly underground or along the expressways, though there could be a stretch of raised tracks somewhere."

Grand. Tyler wasn't even certain of all the routes. Keelin's spirits sank further until they came to an area he called Uptown.

"This is more like the neighborhood I saw," she told him. "The buildings are similar and look to be the right age. But still . . ."

"Not it," he said for her, and went on.

Dusk was deepening by the time they passed under the Addison station a few miles down and turned onto an angled street. The elevated tracks loomed ahead once more.

Suddenly, something sparked her memory. "This isn't the place. And yet . . ." She gazed around avidly.

"And yet what?" he asked, his tone hopeful.

What was it about the area? she wondered as the Jaguar came to a stop amid a sea of other cars where three streets crossed one another.

"Six corners!" she said excitedly. "That's what's familiar."

"Cheryl crossed a three-street intersection?"

"Aye!"

"Why didn't you say so?"

She frowned at him. "But I just did. Is it a help?"

"A real big one," he answered, sounding energized by the information. "Only a few angled streets run across the north side. That cuts down on the number of possible stations."

But unfortunately, they were only able to reach three more possible areas by dark. When Keelin suggested she probably wouldn't be able to recognize the area at night, Tyler conceded they'd best return home and start out again at first light. He headed the Jaguar for North Bluff.

And so that she wouldn't have to think about the woman waiting for them at his home, Keelin considered the information Skelly had provided her.

"Have you thought about who might want to hurt you through your daughter?" she asked.

"I've thought about little else," he conceded. "I just don't know. I might not be the easiest person all the time, but I am honest."

Honest? When he'd pretended his ex-wife was dead and had forbidden her contact with their daughter?

As if he could read her mind, he added, "Under normal circumstances."

Wondering what exactly had been the circumstances that had come between him and Helen, she again pushed the thought away.

"What about a business rival?" she asked.

"My business dealings are squeaky-clean."

"Would that matter if someone kept losing money because of you . . . say, Nate Feldman?"

He gave her a look she could feel even in the dark. "How do you know about Feldman?"

Since mentioning Skelly would probably set him off, she chose to hedge the question. "Through newspaper articles. I read he lost several lucrative contracts to you in the past few years."

"That's the way the business world works. I mean, there's nothing unusual about one company succeeding over another again and again."

"But how do you know this Feldman separates his business from his personal feelings?"

"I don't," he admitted. "Come to think of it, Feldman approached me yesterday morning, right before you did. He congratulated me on the Uptown deal . . . then warned me I wouldn't be so lucky on the

Michigan Avenue project. Said he had the upper hand on that one.''

''Could he have meant Cheryl?''

''Actually, he said something about a lawsuit my company's tied up in. And he doesn't even know Cheryl.''

''You *are* certain?''

''Why?''

''A photograph in one of those newspaper articles... Cheryl was at the site of a building's christening... and so was Feldman.''

Even with only the passing streetlights illuminating the inside of the car, she could see Tyler's frown.

''I was tied up with formalities that day, so it's possible that he spoke to her without my knowing it. But enough to get her to trust him?''

''Maybe that ceremony wasn't the only time they met,'' she mused. ''What if Feldman made it a point to seek Cheryl out sometime later?''

''Bastard!'' he exploded, hitting the steering wheel with the flat of his hand. His horn beeped, and surprisingly enough, the blast settled him down. ''That'd be his style, all right. On the surface, he's all pressed and polished. But underneath...Feldman warned me that there would be 'no holds barred on this one.' ''

Keelin shivered. She could tell Tyler was seriously considering his chief business rival as a suspect.

''Does anyone else have reason to want you hurt?'' she asked. ''Business or personal?''

''Other than my ex-wife?'' His laugh was bitter. ''How about my business partner? Brock wants out of L&O Realty as of yesterday. Seems I'm holding him back.'' Again, the caustic laugh. ''It seems the people I get closest to all want out, including my own daughter. Maybe I'm a worse human being than I ever realized.''

''Whoever has Cheryl is the worse human being,'' she assured him.

When he didn't respond, she let it go. Tension was already thick between them, and they weren't far from Tyler's house. She recognized the dome-shaped temple that lit up a brilliant white against the night sky.

The sky. Illumination from the city skyscrapers reached even this far, dulling the blanket against which the stars lay. At home, she had but to step from her cottage on a clear night to feel as if she were crowned with heavenly jewels.

A wave of homesickness washed over her, and she wondered how Da was faring. She offered a quick prayer for her father's physical recovery and for her own success in giving him a gift that would bring him peace of mind.

Then she worried about her own peace, for she wondered if she would get any at Tyler's home. Not if his ex-wife could help it, she was certain. But upon arrival, she noted no other vehicle in the driveway and had to admit to her relief. Though she'd stood up for the woman's rights to have a relationship with her daughter, she didn't care for Helen Dunn.

''Looks like my ex got tired of waiting to hear about the daughter she professes to be so worried about,'' Tyler said.

''You did try to banish her from the house. Perhaps she took you at your word.''

''Helen does exactly as Helen wants.'' Then he muttered more to himself than to her, ''More likely, she went seeking some male company.''

His comment offered Keelin a hint at what might have gone wrong in their marriage. Had Helen fallen for another man? She imagined that when they were first married all those years ago, Tyler had been just getting started in business. Perhaps he had neglected his young wife too often . . . not that there was an excuse for infidelity.

"You must be starving," he said as he opened the front door. "I never did heat up that food I promised."

"I could use a bite," she admitted, though her appetite wasn't what it should be.

Worry about hunger was the last thing on her mind. Too much else had happened to disturb her. Being together alone in his house brought back clearly what had passed between them earlier. Her in his arms. The sensual demand he'd stirred in her . . . then had extinguished as easily with his harsh attitude toward his ex-wife.

Tyler Leighton was a complex man, she told herself. She'd best not get too close.

"Freshen up if you want," Tyler was saying. "I'll have something on the table in fifteen minutes."

After racing up the stairs to Cheryl's room, Keelin was ready in five minutes. Wondering if Skelly had tried to reach her, she thought to ease her cousin's mind if he was worried about her whereabouts. She called him at home, expecting his machine to answer. But when the ringing was cut off, it was her cousin at the other end.

"Skelly, 'tis Keelin."

"Hey, cuz, I was about to send a posse after you. Where'd you disappear to?"

"North Bluff. Tyler Leighton's home." The pause at the other end telegraphed her cousin's disapproval. "I thought it a good idea to get closer to his daughter." She added, "I already had another contact with Cheryl."

"How so?"

She quickly brought Skelly up to date about the dream and the search, leaving out the more personal details between her and Tyler and skipping over the surprise visit from the dead for the moment.

"And we'll be out looking for the area again in the morning," she finished.

"You're staying in his house for the night?"

"I am."

Skelly didn't try to hide his sigh of disapproval. "You are a big girl, so I suppose you know what you're doing. Just promise me you'll be careful around Leighton."

Her cue to fill in some details. "Skelly, there's been a development." She wasn't certain if telling him would worry her cousin less . . . or more.

"What kind of development?"

"Helen Dunn is alive and well."

"Helen as in Leighton's supposedly dead wife?"

"The same. Helen was here earlier. Skelly, Tyler's been paying off his ex-wife to play dead."

A low whistle at the other end alarmed her. "I asked my research assistant to look into possible divorce records, but she got pulled off that to work on a big story. *This* is big."

Remembering what her cousin did for a living, she hoped she hadn't made a mistake in confiding in Skelly. But before she could caution him that she expected the news to stay strictly between them, she realized she wasn't alone.

The hair at the back of her neck rose as she twisted around to see a glowering Tyler looming over her, his pale eyes as cold as frosted steel.

Chapter Seven

"Keep the information to yourself, Skelly, please," Keelin said, her expression revealing her guilt. "I must hang up now."

Tyler didn't wait until the receiver hit the cradle before saying, "I have to be the stupidest man on earth."

"You aren't stupid—"

"Then what do you call my believing you?" He closed the gap between them. She was sitting on his daughter's bed, for chrissakes. Betraying Cheryl. Betraying *him*. "You swore to me that you weren't hand in glove with your sleazoid-reporter cousin, and I bought it."

"Surely you don't think I was giving Skelly information for another story on you?"

"Just stop this!" He grasped her arm and brought her to her feet. "Stop playing the innocent. I've had enough for one day!"

All the color drained from Keelin's face, and she stared up at him with wounded eyes as if she were the injured party. Her pulse jumped in her throat. Mesmerized, he moved his free hand to her neck, slid his thumb along the center of the slender column until he found the echo of her too-rapidly beating heart.

"The least you could do is be honest with me after I've caught you in your lie."

Her lips trembled. "I have been honest."

Her response was forced, and he sensed she was afraid of him. The same way Helen had been afraid when he'd caught his ex-wife in *her* lies . . .

But Keelin isn't Helen, a small voice inside him insisted.

He snatched his hand away and tightly contained his anger. Not to mention his disappointment.

"Now you're going to tell me I imagined the conversation you just had with your cousin, is that it?" he mused in a much calmer tone. "You didn't waste any time filling him in on my business."

"I merely rang Skelly to reassure him . . . let him know where he could find me."

Fool that he was, he wanted to believe her. He even half did. But he also knew what he'd overheard.

"And Helen's name just happened to pop up in that conversation."

"Not exactly. Skelly had warned me about you because he couldn't find any information about your late wife's death. No obituary. So he thought...maybe..."

"That I did away with her?" The irony striking him, Tyler laughed—he couldn't help himself. Anger tempered by black humor, he said, "So the whole time you've been helping me, you thought I was a murderer?"

"No, of course not. I never believed that, not even before I met your ex-wife." Her forehead furrowed, she moved closer and placed a placating hand on his chest. "I was only hoping to ease my cousin's mind so that he would not worry about me," she insisted. "That was all, Tyler. I swear you can trust me."

"Can I?"

Could she feel the way his heart was beating unevenly beneath her fingers? Could she sense how much he wanted to believe her? Was it possible that even now he might be fooling himself?

Just in case...he tested her. "Then prove it," he said in a low voice, inching closer.

How far would she go to *prove* her innocence? Would she try to entice him with her lips? Her body?

When Keelin backed off, disappointment so clearly written on her features, chagrin filled him and he felt like an idiot.

"If you really do not *want* to believe me," she said coolly, "then I shall leave your house now and never look back."

Keelin decided she was finished with trying to convince Tyler Leighton of her good intentions. Unless he stopped her, she would find Cheryl with Skelly's help and deliver the girl into the hands of the local constables rather than to her father, she vowed, even as she fought the frustration...and something that went far deeper.

Tyler's expression changed, but he said nothing. She crossed her arms over her chest. She would give him about two minutes to decide...and then she would leave.

Heartsick, she counted the seconds.

With only a few seconds to spare, he finally said, "Perhaps I was mistaken."

"Mistaken?" she echoed.

"All right. Maybe I was out of line."

Figuring that she'd gotten more of an apology than Tyler had cared to offer, she was satisfied. Taking a deep breath, she let her arms fall to her side. "I am exhausted. If you'll leave—"

"What about dinner?"

Anything that she put in her mouth now would turn to cardboard, she was certain. "I find that my appetite has dulled."

"In the morning, then."

"I shall rise at daybreak," she agreed.

Unless another visit with Cheryl woke her first.

BUT CHERYL must have been fast asleep herself, for the only dream that came to Keelin in the wee hours of the morning was of Tyler. Rather, of them together, she fumed, staring at the ceiling in the dark.

In the midst of her sleep, she'd envisioned him kissing her, arousing her, confusing her.

For, while made of flesh and blood, human emotions and passions, she was not a woman to be driven by sheer lust. She believed in the kind of love found in high romance—Romeo and Juliet, Guinevere and Lancelot, Heloïse and Abelard—the utopian state of passion her parents had never found together, sadly enough.

The kind she had only dreamed of finding....

Never mind that all of those epic romances had ended in tragedy, she was certain that equally many real romances ended in happily-ever-after. For some reason, one rarely heard about the good endings. Perhaps they weren't dramatic enough. She believed that genuine and total love—of mind, body and spirit—existed. She was certain her grandparents Moira and Seamus had found that in each other, hence Moira's last wish for her grandchildren.

For all of her adult life, Keelin had been waiting to meet the one man she couldn't live without... and according to the McKenna legacy, she was fast running out of time.

But that man simply could not be Tyler Leighton, she decided. Not a man who could deny his child a mother.

But he was also a man who would do anything for his daughter, an inner voice argued. He was a man capable of loving another well, perhaps even more than himself.

She had no doubts that Tyler loved Cheryl with his whole being, that he would do anything to rescue his daughter. He was even trying to trust *her* despite his cynicism and what must have seemed just cause. Tyler was not an unfeeling man, merely a misguided one.

So what was it about him that got to her on a very basic level? The men of Éire with whom she'd kept company had been quite different. Mostly charming and fun-filled, uncomplicated. So why had she never fallen for one of them? Why did she now obsess on a man of dark secrets and passions?

She was still thinking on it when the first gray of dawn stole into the room. Resigned, she rose from the futon. Ten minutes later, she was ready to get started.

When she descended to the first floor, Tyler was already waiting. Rising from a living-room chair that faced the stairs, he came toward her. If he harbored any anger from the night before, she couldn't tell. He seemed calm enough. He even looked better rested than she until they drew closer. Then she noted the puffy flesh below his eyes that indicated he might not have slept so well, after all.

Had he lain awake thinking of his daughter half the night?

"Any dreams?" he asked.

Her pulse thrumming, she lied, "None that would interest you." And felt the heat rise along her neck and steal into her cheeks.

He stared at her for a moment, and though she was certain he noticed, he didn't comment. Instead, he said, "We'd better get going, then. I figured we could grab some coffee and whatever you want to eat at a fast-food joint along the way."

Though her stomach growled its disappointment, she said, "No hurry."

Tyler took her at her word. They were into the city before picking up coffee for him and tea and an English muffin stuffed with bacon and scrambled egg for her. He drove while she ate. Neither talked, yet for once Keelin didn't sense any negative tension emanating from Tyler. He seemed to have put aside his suspicions and resentments for the moment and was concentrating on the music from a CD. Vivaldi's *Four Seasons*.

Keelin was taking a last sip of tea by the time they arrived at the first of their six-corner intersections in sight of an elevated track.

"Here we are," he announced, turning down the music. "Clybourn, Halsted and North Avenue."

Keelin looked around. "Too upscale," she pronounced.

And the next neighborhood was too poor, too near the city's projects.

They kept on and soon crawled northwest on Milwaukee, one of the angled streets, trapped in the morning rush hour. Keelin's mind wandered to Helen.

"Your ex-wife's vehicle wasn't in the driveway this morning, either." She wondered if it had been there at all during the night, or if Helen had found that male company Tyler had suggested. "Is Helen an early riser or did she give up on staying at your house?"

"Helen gives up on anything that takes work."

Like their marriage? she wanted to ask.

"Then you haven't heard from her?" she queried instead.

"Not a word. And that worries me. She wouldn't have stuck her nose in where it didn't belong for nothing."

"What do you think she hoped to get out of the situation?"

"Maybe she decided to sell her story to one of your cousin's competitors."

Keelin chose to ignore the reference to Skelly. "You don't think she could simply be worried about her own daughter?"

"Helen?" He laughed. "Now, that would be a switch."

She couldn't believe his hard-nosed attitude. "You don't think she loves Cheryl?"

"Helen loves Helen," he said bitterly. "She always managed to take good care of number one. She never burned to be a part of her daughter's life before, and I seriously can't imagine anything's changed."

"If she was so self-absorbed, why did you marry her?"

"I was young and foolish. Love can blind a person. Once."

Keelin was about to argue the point when she glimpsed two free-standing telephones at the edge of the sidewalk to her right. Her heart raced as she glanced around and noted the shop she should have remembered.

Just then, the Jaguar slid to a smooth stop at a major three-street intersection.

"Anything familiar here?" he asked, his voice neutral. He was obviously expecting another negative reply.

"The tattoo parlor," she murmured.

"What?" He glanced back the way they'd come.

Then, her breath caught in her throat, Keelin looked around, transfixed. Her gaze flew from building to building, from the elevated track to the newspaper stand. Her heart pounding, she nodded.

"Keelin?"

"This is it!" She peered behind her at the familiar landscape. "Cheryl rang you from those telephones we just passed."

"You're certain?"

"Positive! I didn't remember the tattoo parlor until I actually saw it."

The stoplight changed, and they were forced to move ahead. Tyler wasted no time in finding a parking spot.

As he fed the meter several quarters, she asked, "So what do we do now?"

"Let's backtrack. Maybe you'll remember something else that'll lead us to the building where she's being held."

She knew that probably wouldn't happen, but she didn't want to argue. Didn't want to see the hope in Tyler's eyes die just yet.

So they started at the telephones and worked back the way Cheryl had run across the intersection. Thankfully, Tyler had thought to bring his daughter's photograph. For the next hour, they went in and out of the few businesses that were open, and he flashed the picture in front of anyone who would look. But all he received for his troubles were blank expressions and heads shaking in the negative. No one had seen Cheryl.

Standing at the six-corner intersection, a grim Tyler asked, "What do you remember right before her calling me?"

"She received change for a dollar to ring you at the newsstand."

They crossed the street, and once at the newsstand, Tyler immediately got the proprietor's full attention with a ten-dollar bill followed by the photograph.

The man didn't hesitate. "Yeah, I remember seeing her."

Keelin's pulse surged as, his voice hopeful, Tyler pressed, "More than once?"

The man shook his head. "Yesterday. She needed change for a phone call. Don't usually do that, but I felt sorry for her."

"Why?" Tyler asked. "Was something wrong with her?"

"Hey, I don't know." The man suddenly seemed nervous. "I just gave the kid change."

Tyler flashed Keelin a quick look and asked, "What direction did she come from?"

"You cops or something?"

"He's the girl's father, and he's worried sick about her," Keelin assured him.

"Runaway, huh? Up the street." He indicated she'd come east on North Avenue.

"Which side?"

"This side. And that's all I know."

"What about *after* she made the call. You didn't see what happened to her then?"

"I run a business here, mister! An' I got customers."

His focus shifted to someone who wanted a newspaper. And Tyler drew her aside.

"Are you sure you can't remember details about the building or the street Cheryl came from?"

"All I remember is her passing a couple of lads smoking an illegal substance on a stoop."

Tyler took a deep breath and pressed her. "So the building she ran out of was large?"

"I couldn't say how large," she admitted. "Though it did have at least three flats. She was so..." She didn't want to say *terrified*. He was upset enough. "Cheryl didn't truly focus on anything until she arrived at this area."

Or at least, Keelin hadn't. She remembered instead the girl's heartbeat, the knot in her stomach, the sheer panic that had enveloped her.

"How far did she run?"

Keelin shrugged. "Several blocks."

"At least we know which direction to look in."

As they crossed the street to the Jaguar, Keelin eyed a series of banners set high on the light posts that identified the area as Wicker Park.

For the next half hour, they drove around the neighborhood's side streets. Keelin gazed at two- and three-story buildings, as well as at larger apartment buildings side by side with old homes of cut stone or brick that once must have been considered mansions. The diverse elements and transitional condition of the neighborhood suggested that wealthy people no longer occupied them, however. And every time she thought some building looked vaguely familiar, another popped into view that she thought was familiar, as well.

"I just don't know," she said. "The more I look, the more confused I become."

"We need help," Tyler admitted, slowing the vehicle and staring at a beautiful old commercial building, his brow furrowed. "I'm going to take you back to your hotel for a while to rest."

To rest or to sleep? Was he hoping that she would dream yet again, perhaps see the area through Cheryl's eyes?

Glancing at the building that had Tyler's focused attention—it looked to have been recently renovated—she asked, "And what will you do?"

"Go to my office, where I'll call the North Bluff police chief, see if he can get Chicago's finest to cooperate and do a thorough search."

"You're going to tell the authorities about me?" Keelin was horrified. She wanted no contact with the constabulary. That's why she'd gone to Tyler in the first place. Her pulse surged, and her mouth went dry at the thought of being questioned . . . and, no doubt, being held in suspicion.

"I'll be careful what I tell them."

"Trust me . . . they won't believe you," she said, suddenly feeling desperate. *Trapped.*

"All right. I won't involve you at the moment. I'll say that *I* scoured the area, acting on a hunch."

Thinking Tyler sounded as if he actually did have a hunch of some sort, relieved that she wouldn't be held up to ridicule again, she relaxed. His attention was still absorbed in the renovated building as the traffic before them began to move.

"We have the green," she murmured.

His attention snapped back to the street, and he moved the vehicle. "I'll tell whomever I deal with that I showed Cheryl's photo around until the guy at the newsstand recognized her," he went on. "I'll have dozens of copies made so they can use them to identify her."

"And if the Chicago authorities refuse to help?"

"Whether they do or don't cooperate, I'll still get my investigator on it. I'll give Bryant the go-ahead to bring in more men to comb the area. If the police won't do it, *he* can start a door-to-door search."

Keelin nodded. Not that she believed the people living in the area would necessarily cooperate any more than the authorities would. But she also knew that Tyler had to have hope to hold on to, or he would go out of his mind with worry.

And while he was busy setting up the actual search, perhaps she would delve further into motive.

KEELIN FOUND THAT, despite her initial reluctance to come near a computer, she was able to move along the information superhighway—albeit at a crawl—with a bit of instruction. After Tyler had dropped her off at her hotel, she'd freshened up and had taken a taxi straight to the station. Skelly had finished his morning taping and had readily agreed to do a little more digging for her. At the moment, however, she was mourning the fact that she hadn't actually found anything of note.

Skelly popped back into his office, waving a video-tape. "Lookie, lookie."

"You actually found something? You are an amazing man."

"I found a *big* something." He popped the tape into the recorder and turned on the monitor. "Wicker Park rang a bell. I didn't have to go back very far into our video morgue to find the footage."

She watched with fascination as he punched in some kind of code on the equipment. The machine whirred softly, clicked and an image gelled on the monitor.

"...a tragedy in Wicker Park this afternoon," came the newswoman's voice. "An eleven-year-old boy died searching for his missing pet. It happened at this newly renovated Milwaukee Avenue building...."

Keelin stared wide-eyed. The newswoman was standing before the commercial building that had caught Tyler's attention while they were waiting in traffic.

Then the image changed.

"Harry was just lookin' for his lost dog. My son didn't mean no harm to nobody. An' he wasn't doin' nothing wrong. If that stairway wasn't safe, why wasn't it boarded up or something?"

The man speaking was stocky and had salt-and-pepper hair. His face was grief-stricken. And startlingly familiar.

"A question that authorities want answered from L&O Realty, as well," said the newswoman, reporting from the rear of the building.

The stairway in question was now boarded to block entry, but the broken railing on the second landing was still evident. Keelin swallowed hard, imagining a poor child falling to his death on the pavement below, even as Skelly stopped the videotape.

"The man's name is George Smialek," he said. "And he's suing L&O Realty over his son's death."

"Maybe that's not all he's doing," she murmured, excited. She kissed Skelly's cheek and hurried to the door. "Thank you, cuz," she said, picking up his Americanism.

"Let me know if you need something else. This detective work kind of reminds me of why I became a journalist in the first place."

From the doorway, she flashed him a grateful smile before rushing off to share her conclusions with Tyler.

THE CHICAGO POLICE PROVED to be far less cooperative than Tyler had hoped . . . probably because he'd not been convincing enough even though he'd told them his daughter was being held for ransom. Only a single team of detectives would make the rounds of the Wicker Park area looking for anyone who had seen Cheryl. And though the squad patrols would keep an eye open for her, as well, he didn't consider that nearly enough action to find his daughter fast.

Even Jeremy Bryant was being elusive. He'd called the private investigator's office three times so far, but the man seemed to be unavailable.

So it was up to him, Tyler figured, rereading the missive that had been waiting on his desk when he'd returned to the office: *Get your act together—and your money—fast. The kid's one in a "million." I'll be in touch.*

A million dollars!

Not that he wouldn't pay any amount for Cheryl's safe return, he thought, and not that his net worth wasn't far more than a million. The problem was getting his hands on that kind of cash. He could probably scrape together a few hundred thousand in a day or two. He'd already called his broker and, against the woman's advice, had told her to sell what she could. A second mortgage on the North Bluff estate would get him what he needed—as would a sale of his Barrington land—but both would take time. Still, he had his top agent checking on those possibilities for him.

All of his assets were tied up in stocks and property or in the company.

The company. Tyler was reminded of Brock's determination to dissolve their partnership immediately. Would he be willing to come up with several hundred thousand cold cash to make it happen? Though Tyler still wanted to work things out, he knew this was something to consider. In the meantime, he planned on going door-to-door in Wicker Park himself. He didn't count on Keelin's showing up unannounced.

"What are you doing here?" he asked. "Did you—?"

"No dream," Keelin said, deflating the small hope he'd nurtured that she'd have a clearer idea of where his daughter was being held. "But I learned something else that may be important. It has to do with George Smialek."

Caught off guard, he stared at her. "How did you find out about Smialek?"

"My cousin Skelly."

Of course. The mud raker. "What did he tell you?"

"He showed me the news clip about the boy falling to his death on the L&O renovation site in Wicker Park," she said, her expression sympathetic. "How well do you know the father? Is it possible that he wants revenge?"

"I'm sure he'll get it, big-time." Though no settlement, no matter how much money, could bring back a lost child. "You did know he's suing us?"

"Did *you* know he's been keeping a close eye on you personally?" Keelin countered, the claim amazing him.

"What makes you think so?"

"Monday when you left me waiting while you fetched the Jaguar, a man stood in the shadow of another doorway," she said. "He crossed after you into the car park. I had the oddest feeling, but then you drove out and I thought it was just a coincidence... until I saw Skelly's footage. The man was definitely George Smialek. What could he have been up to?"

Figuring out how to plant a ransom note?

Tyler swore under his breath. After telling her about the second note, he said, "Maybe we should ask Smialek about it in person."

He called Pamela and asked her to check the legal documents on Smialek's lawsuit for his address. When she didn't get back to him immediately, he grew fidgety.

Five minutes later, he said, "Wait here and I'll see what's taking so long."

He found his assistant in a close huddle with his partner at the end of the hall. He stopped and stared at Brock's intense expression. His partner seemed to be angry with Pamela about something. What in the world was going on? Denise was Brock's assistant, while Pamela worked exclusively for *him*.

Then Brock spotted him and broke up the secretive huddle. With a curt nod to Pamela, Brock strode into his own office and slammed the door, leaving Tyler puzzled.

Brock had been acting so strangely the past few days. *Desperate* perfectly described the man's emotional balance.

Takes one to know one, Tyler thought, running a hand through his hair.

Desperate enough to kidnap his partner's child? a small voice asked.

He shook the unconscionable thought away and approached his assistant. "So what the hell is Brock giving you a hard time about now?"

Pamela flushed. "Nothing important. Brock and I get along fine. He's just not in the best of moods today. Not for you to worry, okay?"

When had Brock last been in a good mood? he wondered. No doubt, the man was merely taking his dissatisfaction out on the people who worked for them. And Pamela was correct. Getting involved in employee relations was too much for him to handle at the moment.

"Did you find the papers?" he asked.

"Right here."

She handed him the legal documents, and he quickly took note of George Smialek's Wicker Park address.

"Thanks." He handed the paperwork back to her.

"That's it?" Pamela asked, her eyebrows raised.

"All I need. Keep trying to get hold of Bryant for me."

With Keelin at his side, he left the building, his tension mounting fast.

After pulling from the garage a few minutes later, he drove down the city streets like a madman, praying no cop would interfere. George Smialek. A grieving father wanting to give the source of his anguish some of the same. It made sense. If Smialek were the guilty one, he wasn't really after the ransom money—he'd undoubtedly get plenty through the lawsuit—he was after revenge.

Torturing him with Cheryl's disappearance might only be the beginning, he realized with a sick feeling.

Tyler hoped talking would keep his blood pressure down.

"The building on Milwaukee was an old department store that we're renovating into a retail shop and loft apartments," he said. "Harry Smialek's death was a tragedy—but it was a terrible accident." One over which he'd had a few sleepless nights himself.

"The boy was looking for his dog, was he not?" Keelin asked.

He nodded. "He must have thought he heard the mutt in the building. He climbed the construction fence in back and went up the rear porch. The second-floor landing's side rail was in place but apparently not fully secured. Harry must have leaned on it. He fell through. The dog found him and stood guard over his broken body until the next morning."

"How horrible."

Tyler couldn't agree more. He'd arrived on the scene himself before the boy had been body-bagged. Even now, the vision haunted him.

"My crew chief swore that railing had been properly attached."

"Perhaps he was covering for his men's careless-ness. Or his own."

"Someone was sure careless," he agreed. "City inspectors went over the place, found several other things wrong, as well, including an electrical circuit to the retail area that wasn't grounded. I don't understand. I only hire the best, and these men have all worked for me before. It's like I'm cursed or something."

"Or perhaps some*one*..."

Keelin didn't have to finish the thought. When he'd gotten the bad news, he had wondered himself if someone hadn't been out to sabotage the project and give L&O Realty a bad name.

Or him? he suddenly considered. The renovation side of the business was his baby, after all, as Brock had reminded him.

Brock. Surely not. Surely a dissatisfied partner wouldn't chance damaging the reputation of his own company—not when he wanted to split everything, taking both assets and current clients with him.

Arriving in the Wicker Park area, Tyler gathered his scattered thoughts and focused on their present mission. Rather than wander around looking for the unfamiliar address, he stopped to ask directions. And before they even arrived at George's apartment house, he figured they were on a wild-goose chase.

"Wrong side of Damen," he muttered, catching the steering wheel in a death grip. "The newsstand guy said Cheryl came from the opposite direction."

"Perhaps she crossed Damen and circled around," Keelin said, though she didn't sound convinced. "That part of the vision is so shadowy, anything is possible.''

Tyler pulled up before a six-flat building with a front stoop and wondered if Keelin could be right.

Chapter Eight

George Smialek lumbered to the door on unsteady bare feet, never expecting the high-and-mighty owner of L&O Realty to be on the other side. Him and that same little chippy he'd been dragging around lately.

"What're you doing here?" he thundered, taking a swig of beer.

He'd been drinking a lot since Harry's death. He'd even lost a good job over the booze. The boss had told him to come back when he decided to stay sober. He weren't going back though, George told himself. When this was over, he and Ida would disappear and he wouldn't ever have to work again.

"We have some things to discuss," Tyler Leighton said.

George snorted. "This ain't your type of neighborhood. Unless you kin make lots of money on it," he amended. "Thinking about buying the building and renovating it?"

"Who is it, George?" his wife called from the kitchen.

He held the son of a bitch's gaze as he yelled back, "The man responsible for our boy's death."

"Mr. Smialek, that's not fair," returned the woman in a lilting voice. "Nor truthful."

He narrowed his gaze, thinking that in her floaty, flowery dress and little boots she wasn't the rich man's usual sort. "That building was his responsibility. Who're you to say?"

"My name's Keelin McKenna. May we come inside for a moment? We'd like to talk to you."

She was craning her neck, trying to get a good look around behind him. George all but closed the door with himself wedged in the opening.

"My lawyer says I ain't supposed to talk to anyone connected to the realty company. You wanna settle some money on me, you talk to him."

"We're not here about the lawsuit," Leighton said.

George's hackles rose. "What do you want from me? You already took enough!"

"I'm sorry about your son."

"So you say. Words won't bring Harry back."

Just as words wouldn't bring Leighton's daughter back to him, George thought, giving the rich man a once-over, searching for signs. A subtle tension radiated from him, and his eyes were haunted. George had seen that same look in his own mirror every day for weeks now, ever since they'd buried his boy. But the bastard seemed to be functioning like normal. No creases on his expensive suit. No beard stubble. No telltale smell of alcohol.

George took another swig of his beer. Maybe the rules were different for the rich. Maybe they didn't grieve the same way ordinary people did.

"I can understand your bitterness, Mr. Smialek, but—"

"Cut the crap, Leighton! With your fancy clothes, your fancy house, your fancy car... you don't understand a damn thing about me!"

He got great satisfaction from slamming the door in the big man's face.

"George?"

He turned to his wife, who lurked in the background, her expression worried as Leighton started pounding on the door behind him.

"Smialek, I want to talk to you!" came his muffled demand.

"Tough!" In a softer voice, he said, "Don't worry your beautiful head, Ida, I got rid of 'em."

Her gaze shot to the door. "He's going to cause us big trouble."

"Let him try. He'll be sorry."

George kissed his wife, then drained the can of beer and stalked to the kitchen for another, ignoring the continued pounding... as well as the locked door.

Leighton would be sorry, all right.

He'd get the bastard where it would hurt him most.

KEELIN FOLLOWED TYLER into the temporarily abandoned renovation site. He'd voiced the need to visit the building, as if it would somehow bring him answers about his daughter. Keelin had seen no reason to object.

As she gathered her long skirts to climb the open rear stairs, she thought about the boy who had died there, about the father who lost himself in drink to forget. And as they entered the interior with its sharp smell of new paint and varnish and the more subtle fragrance of cut wood, she tried to determine whether there was some connection between Harry Smialek's death and Cheryl Leighton's kidnapping.

"I don't know," she admitted a short while later, when they stood at a newly installed fourth-floor window that offered an entire vista all the way to downtown. "He was drinking ale like the man who kidnapped Cheryl...."

"Hard to pin a crime on a man over a fondness for beer."

She nodded as she scanned the surrounding rooftops that lay below them. "If only he hadn't closed the door on us before I could see inside, perhaps I could tell better."

"What did you feel?" Tyler urged. "Take a shot at it."

Keelin shook her head. "I can only say what I sensed through Cheryl in the dream," she told him once again. "I don't have the power to read people's minds."

"She's so close... I can almost feel her." His voice was raw with worry. "Out there somewhere... in one of those buildings we can see... sick with fear. A father should be able to keep his child from harm. I would give everything I own to have her safe beside me. Damn it!"

Tyler whipped away from the windows and slumped against the newly exposed brick wall, his shoulders rounded in a gesture of defeat.

"No one has the power to keep another safe always," she assured him. "We can only do our best for those we care about."

Light filtered through the glass, revealing bits of him, just as he only revealed bits of himself at any given moment. But she could see his unguarded expression. She needn't have any special powers to recognize the grief and disappointment that he could no longer hide.

Her need to heal was greater than her hesitation at getting too close to a man who she knew could hurt her at a very deep level.

She stepped into Tyler's personal space and placed her hand gently over his heart, as if she could mute its thunder, could absorb some of his pain. She would take all of it gladly if she could. His warmth captured her even as his fingers closed around her wrist and tightened like a vise, threatening to keep her fast until he willed otherwise.

Her pulse quickened, and her breath caught in her throat.

Then he stared down at her, and she could see that his pale eyes were shiny with unshed tears. He was hanging on to her lest he break. Unable to help herself, she reached up with her free hand and threaded her fingers through his thick hair.

Stroking him.

Soothing him.

Feeling her own insides tremble from the force passing between them.

For a moment, they stood frozen, staring at one another as if seeing each other for the very first time. The moment was magical, a turning point from which they could not retreat. Keelin felt this in her very soul.

Tyler groaned. "I need . . ."

"What is it you need, Tyler Leighton?" she whispered.

His brow furrowed as if he were fighting with himself. "It's not . . . right . . . not when Cheryl . . ." He voiced the objection so low she could hardly hear.

"Tell me," she urged.

"You, Keelin McKenna. I need *you*," he admitted with a deep sigh.

The invitation too great to resist, she stood on tip-toe and softly brushed her mouth across his, the light contact searing her lips. Breath quickening, he drew back, his expression self-accusatory. And though she'd protested the ability to read minds, she sensed he was thinking he should be concentrating on Cheryl. She also sensed the truth of his words that he needed her . . . or at least the comfort she offered.

Keelin wondered if it had been like this between Moira and Seamus . . . this dance between anger and tenderness . . . doubt and faith . . . antipathy and yearning.

She had never before experienced such a whirlwind of conflicting feelings about any man. Fondness at best. Irritation at worst. Certainly not these seething emotions that made her feel alive in every thread of her being, emotions that threatened to overcome her.

She wanted to be overcome, Keelin realized . . . like Juliet had been by Romeo . . . Guinevere by Lancelot . . . Heloïse by Abelard. Like Moira surely had been by Seamus.

Dreams are not always tangible things, but more often are born in the heart.

Her grandmother's legacy stood before her.

They had nothing in common, not even a country. They might not be together next week or even tomorrow. But they could be together now. She'd waited all her life for this, and she refused to let the chance at love—no matter how brief—slip away because of doubts.

"If you need me," she said, her voice trembling, "then know you have me."

Tyler entwined his fingers in her hair and drew her head back as if to see the truth of her words. Her breath caught in her throat, and she wondered how life could be so confused. How two people so far apart could want to be so close. And then his mouth covered hers, and he drew any doubt from her. His tongue filled her as she wanted to be filled in a more tender and aching space.

Her chest rose and fell against his, their heartbeats seeming to match the same too-quick rhythm. He slid his hand down along her neck and captured the fluttery beat through the fullness of her breast. Groaning, he stroked her tenderly, his mouth never leaving hers.

Her breasts tightened and her nipples hardened even before he traced their outline through the cloth. Heat seared her, and her head felt light. She clung to him desperately, her arms winding around his neck, fearing that she might fall if she let go.

Breaking the kiss with an audible groan, Tyler cradled her against his chest, his hands winding around her back, pulling her closer. It seemed as if they couldn't be close enough for him.

Keelin tucked her head between his jaw and shoulder, let her hand drift down his throat. His pulse thudded against her fingers, and when her hand flattened against his chest, her palm captured the uneven beat of his heart. She knew he wanted as well as needed her, just as she did him.

But the time was not right. Not when emotions at another disappointment over his daughter were running so high.

Content to wait, she gave him what she could and hoped that, for the moment, the comfort of her closeness and caring would be enough to see him through the terrible hour.

FOR THE SECOND TIME in his life, Tyler felt emotionally snared. The first time, Helen had nearly destroyed him. Money had presented a partial solution—he'd never really resolved her betrayal—and he'd vowed never to get so close to another woman that he left himself exposed.

Now he'd gone and done it again.

Not that Keelin was anything like his ex-wife. He cared about Keelin McKenna, Tyler realized in amazement. A woman he'd only known for a few days. How had it happened? How had things changed so quickly?

He slid a look over at her. Head resting against the car seat, she seemed to be asleep, her face in repose. A dapple of sunlight played over her features, and he found himself memorizing them. He wondered that he'd ever categorized her looks as ordinary when they were in fact uniquely lovely.

But her looks were not in question here, he reminded himself. Any future between them was. Once they found Cheryl and Keelin completed her family business, she would be heading home to Ireland, he was certain. He would lose her as quickly as he'd found her.

A hard truth to swallow. How many losses could one man endure?

His daughter's innocent face haunting him, he turned his attention back to the busy street. He should be concentrating on Cheryl, not on his own needs. He couldn't fail her. Not again.

Realizing they were nearing his office, he regretted that he hadn't insisted on taking Keelin to her hotel. He was finding it harder and harder to focus on what he had to with her so near him. A flash of her remembered sweetness stirred his insides, and he shifted in the driver's seat.

From the first, he'd experienced a restlessness around her that went deeper than the physical and at times threatened to consume him. Somehow, he'd convinced himself this was the result of his combined distress and animosity and suspicion. He'd really believed Keelin either had something to do with his daughter's kidnapping, or that she was trying to take advantage of his grief.

Now he knew different.

And almost wished he didn't.

SHE COULDN'T BELIEVE IT. Surely they didn't mean to leave her here like this forever.

Tied up.

Gagged.

A prisoner to game shows on the television he'd left on real loud to cover any noises she might make.

Ever since he'd hauled her back to the apartment, they'd kept her locked up in her room. No more pretense. Not after she'd tried running. Not after she'd told them she knew about the ransom.

Since then, he'd been the only one she'd seen and darn little of him, at that.

And now she was alone for who knew how long. He'd told her they couldn't trust her without a guard, not even behind a locked door. So he'd tied her to a chair in the living room. Her hands were already going numb. And the cloth tape across her mouth threatened to choke her.

If she barfed, she'd suffocate—she'd seen that happen in an action movie once—so she wouldn't throw up. She would sit very still and breathe slowly through her nose.

She would pretend that everything would be all right. That they would come for her and take her to her dad. That he'd pay anything to get her back.

She prayed hard that he would as hot tears escaped her eyes and blurred her view of the church steeple across the street.

A SENSATION roving over her face and lingering at her mouth made Keelin open her eyes and meet Tyler's gaze. For the first time since they'd finished the greasy fast-food lunch they'd purchased and had nearly swallowed whole before leaving the Wicker Park area, she was fully awake. She stared at him, wondering at his odd expression. When she realized he noticed, she let her lids drift half-closed, then placed a comforting hand on his thigh.

"Don't fall asleep again," Tyler said, his voice a bit gruff. "We're here."

He turned the Jaguar into the garage across from L&O Realty and waved to the attendant.

Hesitant, she murmured, "I...had another dream."

"Cheryl?" He sounded anxious. "She's all right?"

"I do not believe they've hurt her."

"What did you see?"

"The television." She hoped he wouldn't probe more deeply. She couldn't tell him the circumstances. He would go mad if she revealed that Cheryl was bound and gagged. She couldn't do that to him. "Some game show."

"She hates game shows."

"I know."

"What else? Was anyone with her?"

"She was alone." Waiting. Trying not to panic. Keelin couldn't tell him that, either. "'Tis a pity I could not see more."

"Nothing?" he asked, unable to hide his disappointment.

Nothing she could tell him.

Or was there?

The thought fled as her stomach twirled when Tyler sped up the ramp too fast and squealed around the corner to his assigned parking spot. She suspected that he was releasing his frustration with his vehicle. By the time he cut the engine, she was wide-eyed and sitting up straight. She wanted to comfort him again...if only she knew how.

They left the car and made for the stairwell.

"So what now?" she asked softly.

"What is it *you* think should happen?"

She gazed at him with empathy. "I know what I wish would happen. I would like to be able to see the faces of the people holding Cheryl hostage."

"Yeah, but you're awake, and like you said, you only see through dreams," he said, stirring a memory in her.

"Unfortunately, I can't fall asleep on command or even guarantee a vision when I do." She was reminded of her disappointment when she'd awakened that morning.

Curbside, Tyler waited for a break in traffic. "We're amateurs at this. Too involved to be objective. Damn

Jeremy Bryant! What good is having a private investigator if he's going to be elusive just when I need him. Maybe Pamela's reached him by now. I'll check on it first thing.''

He placed a hand in the middle of her back as they walked across the street. Distracted, she was thinking of the time Moira had told her about lucid dreaming. Dreaming when she was awake. *Controlled* visions. Too bad she'd never explained how to go about it, Keelin thought.

As they entered L&O Realty, Tyler returned but didn't initiate greetings with his employees. And once upstairs, he ducked into his assistant's office but came right out.

''Alma, have you seen Pamela?''

The middle-aged woman shook her head. ''She left like a whirlwind a short while ago. Maybe she went to lunch. She usually lets me know, but not today.''

Tyler shrugged. ''Tell her I want to see her the moment she returns. Keep anyone else out,'' he added. ''We're not to be disturbed until I tell you otherwise.''

''Yes, Mr. Leighton.''

Glancing from him to Keelin, the receptionist wore a knowing and somewhat smug look. Keelin's face flared with color, and she was glad to escape into Tyler's office. What she suddenly wanted was for him to lock the office door and take her in his arms again. Maybe then she wouldn't feel so badly about not telling him all of the dream. She almost got up the courage to approach him and make the first move when a commotion outside the door stopped her cold.

''I tell you he'll want to see me,'' came a familiar female protest.

"He said not until he told me otherwise," Alma returned firmly in a raised voice.

But Keelin heard the clack of high heels directly outside his office. She exchanged looks with Tyler. Heaving a sigh, he opened the door. Vivian Claiborne teetered and nearly fell inside.

"Tyler, there you are," she cooed.

He looked over her shoulder—the receptionist was coming after the woman—and said, "That's all right, Alma. I can give Miss Claiborne a moment of my time."

"A moment?" Vivian pouted. "I remember when you gave me all afternoon and then some." Suddenly, as if just noticing Tyler hadn't been alone, she told Keelin, "Oops. Pretend you didn't hear that, dear," and waved her off as if Keelin were a hired servant.

Alma gave Tyler a look of disgust and went back to her desk. Likewise, Keelin turned away and wandered over to the windows. Her shoulders stiff, she chose the view of the park over the green-eyed blonde, hoping to keep herself calm. First, the dream she couldn't work up the nerve to tell Tyler about... and now, this intrusion.

She pressed her forehead to the cool glass, barely hearing Tyler's, "What do you want, Vivian?"

For below her, she saw Pamela Redmond rushing into the park. Her topknot bobbing, Tyler's assistant was looking over her shoulder as if she feared being followed.

"I thought it only right that I be the first to give you my condolences," Vivian was saying.

Keelin watched Pamela approach a bench where a man turned to greet her. Brock Olander. Keelin supposed they must be going to lunch together.

When Tyler asked, "You've heard something about Cheryl?" she tried to keep her attention on the conversation in the room, but below, Pamela seemed to be yelling at Brock.

"Not your brat, Tyler. Your business."

"Say what you came to say and leave."

Brock grabbed Pamela by the shoulders and drew her down to the bench. She tried wresting herself away, but he pulled her to him for an intense kiss.

"Testy." Vivian ran her French-manicured fingernails up Tyler's tie in a gesture of intimacy. "Though it must be difficult for a man with your determination and drive to lose—and so big."

"Lose what?" His patience, for one, Tyler thought.

"Why, the North Michigan Avenue project, of course. Nate Feldman was awarded the contract this morning," Vivian answered gleefully, dropping a bombshell that rocked him.

He hadn't thought the matter would be decided so soon. Perhaps there was some mistake . . . not that he had the energy to do anything about it.

Staring at the woman who had been his lover for nearly six months, he was disgusted with himself that he'd been such an idiot. He hadn't been able to see exactly how mistaken he'd been until he compared her with Keelin, of course. Vivian had always sworn she liked his daughter, but he'd seen through that particular act. That should have been a big clue as to her nature.

"You do enjoy being the harbinger of bad news."

"Only for *you*," Vivian stated, her smile nasty. "You might not have properly appreciated me when you had the chance, but Nate certainly does."

"You and Nate?" Now, there was an interesting development.

"Jealous, darling?"

"Hardly. I'll give the man my condolences the next time I see him." He watched her complexion pinken. "Wake up, Vivian. Nate undoubtedly thinks he can get information on my business from you, but when he realizes how slim the pickings are, he won't have any more use for you."

The pink deepened to an unbecoming ruddy tone. "I won't be made a fool of by any man!"

"Don't make statements you can't live up to," he suggested. "Two ex-husbands have already put the lie to those words."

Her face wreathed in fury, Vivian barked, "I'll make you regret that, Tyler, if it's the last thing I do!"

The blonde aimed a hateful glare over his shoulder—at Keelin—before spinning on her high heels and tromping out of his office, slamming the door behind her.

And Tyler wondered how he'd been fooled into believing Vivian had been even a little bereft when he'd broken off their affair.

"Sorry about the interruption," he said, turning to Keelin.

When he noted her expression, however, he didn't continue. She was staring at him as if she were looking at something unpleasant.

"How could you speak to her that way?" she asked in a subdued voice.

Maybe he had been a bit hard on Vivian, but the woman had asked for it, coming here to gloat. "She's not worth your sympathy, believe me. Vivian takes care of Vivian first. I'm not even certain if anyone comes second.''

"You said something similar about Helen.''

"So I have rotten taste in women.'' The words were out of his mouth before he had time to think. "Keelin, I'm not including you—''

"Don't.'' She raised her hand as if to ward off any advance.

He considered for a moment. He could force the issue, assure her she was different. Or he could let it go. Let *her* go. Maybe that would be for the best. To let go now.

That's the coward's way out, a small voice inside his head insisted.

Undecided, he wavered for a moment, then finally said, ''I have to make a few calls.''

"Yes, your business, of course,'' she said, her expression unsettled, her tone flat.

"Calls about Cheryl,'' he clarified, thinking he'd also better talk to Brock.

Maybe he could make a deal, agree to split the company as Brock wanted if his partner would give him or at least lend him the part of the ransom money he hadn't yet been able to raise.

Seeing that Keelin had already started for the door, he asked, ''You're not leaving?''

"I need some fresh air.'' Her gaze unflinching, she said, ''I have some thinking to do. I shall return, however.''

He watched her go, then, rather than immediately picking up the telephone, he sauntered to the windows facing the park and waited for her to show. When she did, his insides twisted, for he imagined she appeared too vulnerable. A few hours ago, that's the

last word he'd have used to describe Keelin Mc-
Kenna... but now everything was different.

Or would be if he'd let it.

Only he wasn't certain he could.

KEELIN NEEDED to renew her communion with nature. She also needed to force Tyler Leighton from her
mind for a while. Unfortunately, her approaching
Lincoln Park accomplished neither. She stared ahead
at the flower beds and trees, but rather than taking
pleasure in them, she could think only about the way
she'd thrown herself at Tyler.

A man who openly declared he had rotten taste in
women.

And the way he'd spoken to a woman he had once
kept company with... slept with...

Keelin shuddered.

Her uneasiness followed her into the park. She felt
as if someone were physically pursuing her down the
sidewalk, when she knew the only thing wrong was
that her unprecedented actions were preying on her
mind. Still, she clutched the strap of her shoulder bag.

All these years of waiting for the right man... of
wanting to fulfill Moira's legacy... and she'd gone and
chosen a man who either didn't respect women... or
didn't like them.

The scene with Vivian had reminded her of what
Tyler had done to his ex-wife, of how he'd kept Helen
from her own child. She'd conveniently forgotten
about that for a while.

What was she to do now?

The sensation of being followed grew stronger.
Thinking to see Pamela or Brock, she glanced over her
shoulder. But the only people behind her were a

woman pushing a stroller, and behind the young mother, a man wearing a windbreaker, his capped head bent as he adjusted the portable radio clipped at his waist. Nothing to concern herself over.

The man jogged past her at an easy clip. She didn't give him a second glance as her thoughts strayed back to Tyler. He had shown a different, appealing side of himself earlier... strong yet tender... vulnerable yet commanding.

He had enticed her as no man ever had.

What to do?

The dream drifted back into her thoughts, undoubtedly because she was feeling a bit guilty at not having told Tyler. But what purpose would it serve to worry him further? Poor Cheryl tied up and gagged...

She came to a pedestrian tunnel and saw a large lagoon supporting both paddle boats and wildlife at the other end. Perhaps she could find some answers there. At home, Lough Danaan had soothed her more times than she could remember.

Keelin turned and made her way down the dark, dank tunnel. Walls covered with graffiti. Lights broken. Litter underfoot. Halfway through, she looked to the opening ahead. An archway of sunlight. A frame for the large brick building that sat before the lagoon.

Her feet slowed.

For a second, the opening was a window, the building a church....

Her concentration was broken by feet beating the path behind her. A jogger. She moved to one side to let the person pass and so was startled when a body rammed her, knocking her down. Her shoulder bag went flying.

"Pardon me!" she said, getting a glimpse of sunglasses below a billed cap and a portable radio clipped to the man's waist.

She didn't see whatever smacked into the side of her head.

...out the ... gotten all the ...
... found a bullet wedged ... gunshot today, next
to be shot a week.
... the Leigh ... surprise, ... for later, she ...
him?

Chapter Nine

"This is your only warning," came a gravelly and obviously disguised male voice as Keelin noticed the man wasn't wearing jogging shoes. "Stop trying to help Leighton unless you want to end up food for the fish in Lake Michigan."

Attempting to rise, she reached out and grabbed his wrist, then pulled herself up until he shoved her hard with his free hand. Something gave. She flew into the concrete wall, the object clutched in her hand. Too dizzy to stay on her feet, she sank back to the ground. And though she tried to get a better look at the man as he tore down the dark tunnel, she could hardly focus.

Dazed, her heart beating too fast, she leaned her head against the wall and took deep breaths. She was going to have one grand headache. Slowly, she recovered her shoulder bag, which lay several feet away. Then she worked herself up to her feet. Her surroundings whirled, and her stomach churned. She was definitely both dizzy and queasy, so she stopped moving. Wondering how she was going to get herself back to Tyler's office—crawl, perhaps?—she thought she was hearing things when her name reverberated down the tunnel.

"Keelin!"

"Tyler?" Bile rose to her throat, and she instantly regretted trying to speak at all.

"Are you all right?" he demanded, twirling her around.

The motion was too much for her head and stomach. Doubling over, she lost her greasy lunch... all over Tyler's expensive leather shoes. To his credit, he didn't even utter a sound of disgust, merely supported her weight. When her world stopped spinning, she carefully inched herself into a standing position.

"Are you all right?" he demanded in a low, urgent voice, his arms cradling her. "What did he do to you?"

"Hit me in the head with something," she said, groaning. "How did you know?"

"I was watching from my office window. The bastard was acting suspicious. I could tell he was watching you. I got down to the street as fast as I could. Apparently, not fast enough. He was disappearing into the tunnel before I could even cross to the park."

"I could use some air."

With care, he guided her back the way they'd come, then led her to a bench and made her sit. Only then did he try scraping the leftovers of her lunch off his shoes with a plastic bag he pulled out of a trash can.

"I think I owe you a new pair of shoes," she said.

"I'd rather have a description of your mugger to give to the police."

"He was not a mugger... didn't try to take my shoulder bag," she said, gripping the leather strap. "He must be the man who has Cheryl."

"What?"

"He said—" she thought hard to remember "—that this was my only warning to stop helping you."

Tyler threw the plastic back into the trash and said, "Don't move!" Then he headed back for the tunnel.

She held her protest. She watched him disappear, figuring he was on a fool's errand. Her attacker had too much of a head start, and there were several directions to choose from on the other side.

Sure enough, Tyler quickly reappeared.

"He's long gone. Did you get a close look at his face?"

Keelin shrugged. Everything was fuzzy. "His hat was pulled low, and he was wearing sunglasses. And street shoes."

She had the feeling there was something else... something that Tyler would want to know... but the thought was elusive. Her head was starting to pound. She looked down at the object still clutched in her hand.

"This is his," she said, showing him a watch with a broken gold band.

But there was more, wasn't there? Thinking about it only made her head throb.

Taking the watch from her, he said, "A Rolex." He looked at the back. "'Darling,'" he read, "'to our future.' No name or initials. But whoever was wearing this must have money."

"Not George Smialek, then," she said. What she'd seen of his apartment hadn't reflected the money it would take to buy a Rolex. "Oh, Tyler, I'm sorry I cannot tell you more."

"No, *I'm* sorry," he said, slipping the watch into a trouser pocket. "This never should have happened to you. My letting you help only put you in danger."

"Let me? I would have tried to find Cheryl with or without you."

"I believe you would have," he said, something like awe in his tone. He looked down the street. "Where's a taxi when you need one?"

"Your office is barely a block away."

"But the emergency room is a bit farther."

"No hospital. I'm fine." But the moment Keelin stood, she felt weak-kneed. "Perhaps I could use a place to lie down for a few minutes...."

"You could have a concussion. First, the emergency room, then the lie-down."

She knew arguing wouldn't do any good. Besides, she didn't have it in her, so she let Tyler hail a taxi and take her to nearby Grant Hospital. Fortunately, a lump on her head and a headache were the only things the intern who checked her over could find wrong with her. He gave her an analgesic for the pounding and a frozen gel-pack for the goose egg. He suggested she get some rest, but that Tyler not leave her alone. Someone needed to check her on a regular basis to make certain her pupils stayed evenly dilated and that she could be roused every so often.

Just in case.

After bundling her into another taxi and giving the driver the L&O Realty address, Tyler said, "I hope you don't mind resting for a while on one of our couches. I have a few things to take care of before leaving for home."

"About Cheryl," she said knowingly.

"I have to get my hands on that money. This guy means business."

Something he didn't have to tell her. Her aching head said it all. If the kidnapper would hurt her to keep her out of the way, what would he do to Cheryl if Tyler couldn't gather together the million dollars fast enough?

As TYLER SETTLED Keelin on the couch in the conference room, he couldn't help but regret her involvement in his problems. But that would have to end.

"Keelin, from now on, I want you to stay out of the line of fire."

"I'm in this with you, Tyler."

"But you shouldn't be."

"I must."

"I won't have you getting hurt . . . or worse."

"I will not have you telling me what to do," Keelin protested, rising on her elbows. "I must see that Cheryl is safe . . . so that I can be at peace."

"That sounds pretty ominous."

"Sit." Keelin carefully swung her legs to the floor and straightened, then patted the cushion beside her.

Tyler complied.

And she went on, "I told you about the first time I had one of my night terrors."

"The friend you lost."

"I vowed then never to involve myself again. For a decade, I wasn't even tested. Any such dream-visions were not of the desperate sort."

Tyler had the feeling he knew where this was going. He swung an encouraging arm around her shoulders and pulled her close. "Go on."

"I was still living with my family at the time. A Traveler by the name of Gavin Daley did some chores for us. I fed him a good meal and gave him some of Da's old clothing, then saw him on his way. That night, I dreamed through his eyes. A true nightmare," she whispered.

"You said he was a traveler? You mean a visitor?"

"A person whose only home is his horse-drawn caravan," she explained. "Many don't like the wandering people. They chase Travelers off their land...break up their camps...sometimes hurt them."

"And you saw someone trying to hurt this Gavin Daley?"

Keelin shuddered. "Aye, that I did. A group of lads coming home from a night at the local pub full of drink and meanness overturned his caravan. They were laughing when Gavin escaped. When he saw what they had done to his home, he grabbed one of the young men and threw him. The lad's head hit the wheel, and he sank to the ground unconscious. The others went after Gavin. Out for blood, they were, they chased him down to Lough Danaan. I could see their black looks, hear their shouted curses. I could feel the terror in Gavin Daley's heart." She was trembling as if she'd just experienced the whole thing when she said, "And then I awoke...and did nothing. I did not want to play the fool again, you see."

He squeezed her and gently stroked her hair. "And later you were sorry you didn't."

"The next morning, they found Gavin Daley in the shallows of Lough Danaan. After they beat him, they held him facedown until he drowned. I knew he was in desperate trouble...and I did nothing. That poor man's death is on my soul."

"You're not responsible," he said, turning her so he could look into her face. How could she possibly assume such a burden? He stroked her cheek. "You didn't hold him under the water. And even if you had called the police, they might not have arrived in time to save him."

"But what if the constable had been quick?" Her expression desperate, she demanded, "Do you not see? I chose to hide from my responsibility and now I have a man's death on my conscience. For years, I thought there was no way I could ever forgive myself, but perhaps there is. I did not know your daughter or you, Tyler. So why did I dream through her eyes but for fate giving me another chance? By making certain your daughter is safe, perhaps I can redeem myself. I truly cannot live with another such burden on my soul. Do you not see?" she asked again.

He saw too much. A woman who was afraid. She'd told him so. He hadn't really believed her until this moment. She was a woman who most feared failing others. Feared that she would be unable to carry the burden of responsibility her grandmother had laid across her tender shoulders as a young girl.

And yet she was truly the most fearless, selfless woman he'd ever had the good fortune to know.

"I see," He silently vowed that if he couldn't stop Keelin, he would find a way to protect her. He brushed her lips with his and stroked her cheek again. "I do see."

Her expression lightened. "Good. Good, then."

Tyler untangled himself from her and rose. "Now, you get some rest while I do what I must to raise the ransom."

She nodded and stretched out on the couch again. "Don't forget about me."

As if he ever could.

Tyler followed up with his broker and banker and real-estate staff, checking on Keelin in between. He even called in a few favors, asking for personal loans. No matter which way he added up the liquid assets available to him, however, they didn't come to enough. He was short more than two hundred thousand dollars. He neither had a serious prospect for the Barrington property nor could he remortgage the North Bluff estate until next week at the earliest. He was certain a week would be too late.

It was the business, then.

Swallowing his pride and his anger with his partner, he went to see Brock. The office door was open, and Brock was busy going over some contracts. Tyler knocked on the wooden panel and stood in the doorway until the other man glanced up, his expression immediately darkening.

"Can we talk?" Tyler asked. "About the business."

"You've actually thought about it, then?" his partner asked, sounding surprised.

"I've been forced to..."

Brock's face went blank. "What do you mean?"

"I need to know how much getting out of our partnership is worth to you. Above taking half of the company's assets and clients with you, that is."

Brock indicated Tyler should come in and take a seat. "So make me an offer."

"I need a quarter of a million in cash. Fast," he answered bluntly.

Brock didn't even blink. "How fast?"

"I'm not sure yet."

"You have the rest of the ransom money?"

"I will by tomorrow."

How did Brock know about the ransom when he'd asked Pamela to keep the information to herself? Tyler wondered. She must have told him anyway. But why? She knew he and Brock were at odds. Then he remembered the scene between his partner and assistant at the end of the hall. Pamela had brushed off his concern....

"The kidnappers want a cool million for Cheryl's return," he said in case Brock didn't have all the details. "I don't know when. I don't know where. I only know it's going to be soon."

"And you're not bringing the police in on this?"

"I won't risk my daughter's life."

His soon-to-be ex-partner sprawled back in his chair. After a moment's hesitation, he said, "I think we can work something out...especially if you're willing to hand over the Uptown renovation to me."

And Tyler took his first deep breath in days.

"YOU HAVE COMPANY," Keelin said when they reached Tyler's North Bluff property just after sunset.

Two vehicles were parked under the carport, one she recognized as belonging to Helen.

"Either my ex-wife stole a spare set of keys the other night or she broke in," he muttered, cutting the ignition.

Keelin didn't react to the caustic remark. He hadn't, after all, given Helen Dunn the keys to his home.

After a few hours of rest—she couldn't exactly call her time on his sofa *sleep* since Tyler had checked on her every half hour—plus a shower at her hotel and a fresh set of clothes, she felt decidedly better. As long as she didn't touch the left side of her head carelessly, she reminded herself. Washing and combing her hair had been especially unpleasant.

Tyler raced around the Jaguar before her door was half-open. Continuing to be solicitous, he helped her out. "If you like, you can go right upstairs—"

"I would not sleep," she cut in. "Besides, you need me." When he gave her a questioning look, she kept her gaze steady with his. "Well, is that not what you told me earlier?"

"It was," he said. "But I don't need you to protect me from my ex-wife."

As he opened the front door, she returned, "You are more certain of that than I."

Laughter carried into the foyer from the living room. Tyler stopped short in the double doorway, Keelin at his side. She saw that his ex-wife was entertaining a muscular young man who looked to be in his midtwenties. Thick golden brown hair brushed his high forehead and topped such perfect features that he could have been a model or actor. Half-empty glasses sat on the coffee table, and the two appeared to be enjoying each other.

Tyler's tension was palpable. And Keelin suspected old, harsh memories were surfacing.

Before he could announce his presence, Helen spotted him. "Ah, there you are, Tyler. I was beginning to think you would never come home." She shot a significant glance at Keelin and raised her eyebrows. "Have you heard anything about our daughter?"

"*My* daughter is none of *his* concern."

"Why, that's where you're wrong, darling," Helen stated. "Mr. Weaver is an associate of Jeremy Bryant, the private investigator *you* hired."

"Jack Weaver," the young man said, getting to his feet and crossing the living room, his hand outstretched. "Jeremy had to leave town unexpectedly. The case was one he'd been working on for weeks, and something important broke. He asked me to cover for him here."

Though Tyler seemed reluctant, he shook the young man's hand. "And when was that?"

"A while ago," he said vaguely. "You'd already left your office. Naturally, I assumed you were headed home. So here I am."

"And isn't it fortuitous that I was here to let Mr. Weaver in," Helen said.

"Fortuitous," Tyler echoed. "Question is—how did *you* get in?"

"I *was* married to you for several years, Tyler. Long enough to know where you like to keep things. Finding your spare keys was a snap."

"Well, snap them over here," he insisted, holding out his hand.

"Don't be a bore."

"Don't make me take them from you."

Giving him a dark look, Helen removed the keys from her pocket and threw them at him. "This doesn't mean I'm going anywhere. I already brought my bag upstairs."

"Why are you here, Helen?" Tyler asked as he had the last time.

"I made one mistake turning my back on my child. I'm not about to make another."

They glared at each other long enough to make Keelin uneasy. She tried to smooth things over. "Would anyone like something to drink? Tea?"

"No!" came the unanimous answer.

"What *I* would like," Tyler said, seating himself in a wing-back chair, "is to know what Bryant came up with about my daughter before leaving town."

Weaver shrugged. "Not much. Her friend Tiffany said Cheryl had been upset about something for the past few days. Your daughter wouldn't say what... only that it involved you."

Keelin felt Tyler's ache as if it were her own, and her curiosity on the subject was renewed.

"What did you do to our daughter to upset her enough to make her run away?" Helen demanded.

"Nothing!" Tyler insisted, yet Keelin heard the uncertainty in his denial.

Keelin perched on the other vacant chair and turned to the private investigator. "What about a reference to someone Cheryl knows who happens to live in the city?"

"Jeremy didn't pass on any such information."

"Then why are you here?" Tyler demanded.

"To offer my services to take up where he left off." Weaver pulled out a notebook and pen. "Have you heard from your daughter since you last spoke to Jeremy?"

"As a matter of fact, yes."

Tyler told the private investigator about the ransom notes and about the aborted telephone call. Without explaining how they figured it out, he also told Weaver about the Wicker Park location.

"That narrows it down. What about the Chicago Police Department? Are they on it?"

"Two detectives asking questions. Patrols on the lookout. We need someone going door-to-door, Weaver. I was hoping Bryant could round up a team."

"I don't have his resources. But I could get on the case myself." Weaver made as if to check his wrist, then stopped himself. "I have a couple of hours to work before it gets too late."

Throughout the conversation, Helen had remained quiet, Keelin noted. For all her protestations to the contrary, she seemed oddly uninvolved emotionally for a mother who knew her child was in trouble. She covertly continued watching Helen as Tyler gave Weaver a photograph of Cheryl. The man took down more specifics about the exact streets he should canvas and left.

Tyler warmed up one of the dinners the housekeeper kept in the freezer for him and Cheryl. Helen made no move to leave, but since Keelin didn't have much of an appetite, the meal for two stretched far enough. The table was a hostile environment, with Tyler and his ex-wife doing a good deal of glowering at each other if not actually trading barbs. Directly afterward, Helen volunteered to retreat to the bedroom she'd chosen, leaving Keelin and Tyler alone.

"Would you like some fresh air?" he asked.

Still sensing the leftover tension in the room, Keelin said, "I would love that."

The night was heavenly. In a clear, starlit sky, a nearly full moon shone as they picked their way down the wood stairs to the narrow strand at the base of the bluff. Two Adirondack chairs awaited them.

Tyler pulled the wooden chairs closer together, so when they sat, they were side by side if not actually touching. Keelin laid her head back and stared up at the sky. Listening to the water lap almost at her feet, her face caressed by a sharp lake breeze, she could almost imagine she was home in Éire, sitting on the bank of Lough Danaan.

"Ah, 'tis a wondrous night," she murmured with a sigh.

"And I feel wondrously guilty that I'm not doing something to find Cheryl."

"Don't." She moved her hand from her armrest to touch his. "You've done all that you could."

"I should be knocking at doors in Wicker Park myself."

"You're not a professional," she said. "Jack Weaver is. Perhaps he will earn his fee."

"I hope so. Even if I get the whole million together, that's no guarantee . . ."

That he would ever see Cheryl again, Keelin silently finished for him.

"You must keep your thoughts more positive," she murmured.

An elusive image reached for her, hovering just beyond her conscious mind. But every time she tried to concentrate on it, her head ached.

"If only we could figure out why this is happening, what the villains have against me," Tyler said, turning her attention back to what she could say for certain.

She ticked off the facts as they had them. "A man and a woman are working together. They have an intimate relationship. And they want you to know what it's like not to be in control."

"And the man used to wear a Rolex watch until today," he added.

"Does Nate Feldman wear a Rolex?"

"Knowing Feldman, he probably does."

"And he and Vivian Claiborne are now involved..."

"Vivian sure as hell was thrilled about Feldman getting the North Michigan Avenue contract," he muttered. He paused, then continued. "And there's George Smialek and his wife, Ida. They have the strongest reason to want revenge *and* they live in Wicker Park."

"Mr. Smialek would never be able to afford a Rolex watch, though," Keelin reminded him. Hesitating only a second, she added, "But your partner could."

"I haven't noticed what brand watch Brock is wearing these days, but I can't believe he'd do anything to hurt Cheryl. He's always been so fond of her."

"And she, no doubt, always trusted him."

Tyler swore under his breath. "No! He's so desperate to break up our partnership that he's willing to give me part of the ransom money."

"That doesn't eliminate him." How odd that a man so given to doubt refused to suspect his partner.

"A kidnapper would supply part of the ransom to himself?"

"Wouldn't he have some idea of how much cash you could raise in a short time?"

He swore again. "I know what you're getting at. Don't you think I've considered Brock myself? True, he could be playing along because he'll get what he wants—a clean split and a new chance to prove himself. Maybe that's worth a quarter of a million to him. But the kidnappers are a couple, remember. Brock's not currently married, and none of the women he's dated has any reason to resent me," he said, loyally arguing in his partner's defense.

"Not even Pamela?"

His hand tensed under hers. "What are you talking about . . . ?" His words trailed off. "I *have* seen them in a few intense huddles lately."

"And *I* have seen them kissing."

"When?"

"This afternoon, when Vivian came by," she said. "I was staring out at the park when I spotted Pamela. Brock was waiting for her. If he is the one, he would throw suspicion from himself by offering to help you raise the ransom money."

Silence. She sensed Tyler was taking her seriously.

"Brock was in the park today shortly before you were attacked?" he suddenly asked.

A thrill shot through her. She hadn't made the connection herself. Could Tyler's partner have tried to warn her off?

"He couldn't guess that I would take a walk, though."

"Maybe it was a fluke. He saw his opportunity and took it. He could have parked nearby, could have had a windbreaker and cap inside the car. How long would it take to pull them on?"

"The man *was* wearing street shoes," she admitted. It was possible.

"I know it's reaching," he said. "Besides, Pamela's loyal to me."

"But maybe she's personally committed to your partner."

"Why is it I can't ever trust a woman?" Tyler exploded.

Remembering the suspicion he'd met her with, Keelin was saddened that one woman had so clouded his view of life. "You can trust me."

He turned his hand so that it was cupping hers. "You're the exception to the rule," he said, squeezing her fingers.

Her heart skipped a beat. "You didn't think so at first. Do you look at every woman you meet with the same misgiving?"

"Maybe I do."

"A terrible way to go through life, Tyler. More than a decade has passed—do you not think you could forget whatever happened between you and Helen?"

"Not as long as I live."

He fell silent again, and she wasn't certain he would say more on the subject. Her heart hurt for him. A terrible thing—not being able to trust.

"I suppose you'd need to know more to understand," he said. "And I suppose it's time I told someone. Someone I've come to trust," he added.

Knowing how much that concession cost him, Keelin linked her fingers through his in a gesture of solidarity. "Sometimes, a dark secret can be more of a burden than a person can bear." She knew of what she spoke.

"Helen had an affair," he said bluntly. "I imagine you've guessed that."

"You are a bit transparent there."

"When I met her, she was a moderately successful model. I was in the park on a day she was shooting an ad for a local paper. Like an idiot, I fell instantly in love with the image she was projecting rather than the real woman. And for reasons of her own, Helen decided she wanted marriage to me, despite her ambitions."

An easier way to become rich if not famous? she wondered, though she did not put words to the hurtful thought.

Instead, she leaned toward Tyler across the chair and rested her forehead on his shoulder. His arm slid around her back, his touch thrilling her, making her want to get even closer.

"At first, she seemed happy," he went on. "I encouraged her to keep working if that's what she wanted. Maybe everything came crashing down because she became pregnant too quickly, effectively ending her modeling career."

Keelin splayed a hand across his chest, felt his heart thrum against her palm. "But after the baby was born, she could have gone back to work."

"At first, she didn't want to be pregnant. She was downright hysterical when she found out. We argued . . . and she appeared to accept the situation. After Cheryl was born, she even seemed to be a good mother. For a while."

"Until the affair started?"

"Going off with another man would be bad enough," Tyler said grimly, "but she brought Cheryl along with her on her trysts. Or brought her trysts into our home. And one day, she was too involved with her own pleasure to realize that her two-year-old child had wandered off. That's how I learned about the affair—I came home to a police car at the curb."

"You must have been frantic." Even more so than he was now, she imagined. "What about Cheryl?"

"I'm the one who found her, blocks from home. She could have been killed. It was a miracle that she wasn't even hurt. But after Helen tearfully confessed the sordid details . . . I wanted to kill both her and her lover. I remember wrapping my hands around Helen's throat. . . ."

Keelin swallowed. He must have exerted some superhuman control to resist harming Helen. She herself had felt the tightly leashed ferocity in him more than once. Then again, his daughter was lost to him, as she had been so long ago.

"I couldn't stay married to Helen any longer," Tyler was saying.

"So her affair and the neglect of your daughter are the reasons you were able to secure custody."

He wrapped an arm around her back and pulled her out of her seat as if he needed closeness for courage to finish the story. She gladly settled on his lap, wrapped her arms around his neck and touched her forehead to his temple.

"Helen swore she would fight me," he went on, his tone low. "Considering the circumstances, I didn't think she could win. But she at least would have had visiting privileges, as she so clearly reminded me. Helen demanded an absurd settlement and a yearly stipend that wouldn't end even if she married. If I didn't agree, she said one day Cheryl might just disappear . . . and I would never see my daughter again. I was furious that she would use her own child as a pawn, but I agreed to give her what she wanted. She would get the money . . . but only if she agreed to be dead to her daughter."

Keelin sensed how painful the admission was for Tyler. And yet his confession gladdened her. He had to feel something special for her if he was willing to share the sordid details that he'd kept locked up inside him all these years. And she was glad, for now she understood. He was no monster.

"I never wanted Cheryl to find out what kind of a woman her mother was," he whispered. "I feared it would destroy her. Helen took all of thirty seconds to agree to the deal. I made a pact with the devil and have had to live with the guilt for twelve years."

Suddenly the import of what he'd just admitted hit her. "So Helen threatened to *kidnap* her own daughter?" she asked, her mind already whirling.

"I guess you'd call it that."

"And now someone *has*. Why not your ex-wife?"

"Someone Cheryl trusted," he reminded her.

She pulled back slightly, so she could look into the pale eyes that were for once open and vulnerable.

Why did he do it? Why? Now that I know, everything is ruined.

His daughter's remembered thoughts spinning in her own head, she asked, "Are you certain that Cheryl didn't somehow find out about her mother?"

He sighed. "I can't be certain of anything. Something was wrong between us for a few days before she disappeared. We even argued the night before. Cheryl made accusations... but she wasn't clear about what I'd done. I thought maybe someone had put an idea in her head that Harry Smialek's death was my fault or something. But underneath..."

He didn't have to say that he thought Cheryl might have suspected her mother was alive. But how to know for certain?

"At one time, you knew Helen better than anyone in the world. Could she actually hurt her own child?"

He tightened his arm around her and slid long fingers around the back of her neck. "I don't know. I don't seem to be certain about much of anything anymore.''

Their mouths met in a kiss filled with repressed passion and infinite tenderness. Keelin was moved. Filled with longing, she at the same time wanted no more than this gentle melding. This proof that they were closer than she had ever suspected was possible.

Tyler broke the kiss and sighed. ''Ah, Keelin.''

She pulled his head to her breast. And though his physical warmth stirred her, the emotional bond they were forming was far more potent. He had opened up to her with his deepest, darkest secret as she had to him earlier. Their mutual trust had to mean something.

The words of her grandmother's legacy drifted into her mind: *Dreams are not always tangible things, but more often are born in the heart. Act selflessly in another's behalf, and my legacy shall be yours.*

Love was that legacy, Keelin knew—the unexpected love she felt for Tyler Leighton—though she worried that she had not truly acted selflessly as Moira had advised. She had nearly as much at stake here as did Tyler.

He had his daughter.

She had her very soul.

How long could a love born in the desperation of the human heart last? she wondered. If not for Cheryl's running away, they would never have met. If not for Tyler's grief over his missing daughter, he would not be so open.

What about when the child of his heart was returned to him? Would he have room for *her,* as well? she wondered. Not that it mattered, for as she had told herself before, they were worlds apart.

And yet, sitting in the dark, the lake breezes curling the thin material of her dress up along her legs, wrapped in arms that she never wanted to leave, Keelin couldn't quite see that anything mattered but love.

SOME TIME LATER—Tyler couldn't say how long for certain—he realized that he had dozed off cocooned around Keelin, dazed by her warmth. With awakening came the remembrance that he no longer had any secrets. Uncomfortable at having opened up so completely to the woman in his arms, he felt the need for some space.

And yet, he said, "Keelin, we'd better get inside," as softly as if they'd just made love.

The mental comparison betrayed him, and he grew increasingly uncomfortable as she stretched and wiggled her bottom against him as she slid to her feet. Splashed by moonlight, she seemed dreamy eyed... and yet her smile was a bit distant, not quite reaching her eyes.

He followed her up the stairs to the top of the bluff. They crossed the lawn side by side, and he was careful not to touch her. She seemed equally tentative. An awkwardness hung between them even as they entered the house in mutual silence. As she glided through the dining room, he busied himself locking up the French doors.

"I'd better check the front," he said, brushing by her in the foyer.

He'd snapped the dead bolt in place when he happened to look down. The breath caught in his throat. A plain white envelope sans postage but bearing his name was caught beneath the door. Like a madman, he ripped it free and tore it open.

"Tyler?"

As he unfolded the sheet of pasted letters, he glanced up and their gazes locked. He swore he could feel strong emotions pour from her to him, as if they were psychically united. He felt her support . . . and something far deeper.

Discomfited, he focused on the third ransom note.

The fireworks will go off at Navy Pier at 10:15 Friday night. Wait at the north end of the Crystal Gardens with the goods in a backpack for a trade. Come alone if you don't want anyone to get hurt.

"What does it say?" she asked anxiously.

"Forty-eight hours."

Taking the threat seriously, he refolded the ransom note and slipped it into his pocket. He would have to go alone. That meant he couldn't divulge the details lest Keelin take it into her head to follow him. She was desperate to redeem herself for something that wasn't even her fault.

Better that she live with her past not fully resolved than not live at all.

Chapter Ten

Another dreamless night left Keelin praying that Cheryl had merely been sleeping soundly. The other possibility—that some real harm had come to the girl—was too terrible to contemplate. She rose, staring unseeing at one of the windows where the morning light poured into the bedroom.

Gradually focusing, she stared at the square of brilliance and at the massive tree trunk beyond.

Suddenly another window took shape in her mind.

Tied and gagged, Cheryl had nonetheless been able to *see* the last time Keelin had tuned into her, and she'd been staring at what lay outside the living-room window.

A church steeple!

The image that kept eluding Keelin the day before.

She flew out of bed, pausing when the room shifted slightly, but quickly regained her equilibrium. Her head barely hurt anymore.

Freshening up in record time, she dressed with a renewed sense of purpose. Tyler couldn't keep her from returning to Wicker Park with him! She almost felt like going it alone—taking a taxi—and letting him wonder what she knew.

Almost.

It still galled her that he'd refused to show her the ransom note the night before, and had only revealed the Friday-night deadline. He knew she was committed, for heaven's sake. Never mind that he swore he was only trying to protect her from herself.

She'd believed him when he said he trusted her. So why couldn't he have proved as much?

The smell of fresh coffee assaulted her nose when she left Cheryl's room. Normally a tea drinker, she occasionally indulged in a cup of the stronger stuff. And so she swept into the kitchen and made straight for the mug tree, noting that not only was an exhausted-looking Tyler at the table, but his ex-wife, as well. Nursing a mug of coffee, a belligerent expression detracting from her beauty, Helen was still in her bathrobe.

"Have you heard anything from your Mr. Weaver?" Keelin asked, her voice tight with irritation left over from the ransom-note issue.

She filled a mug, and Tyler's eyebrows shot up as he watched her.

"He's not my Mr. Weaver and yes, he checked in," Tyler groused. "He found a woman who *maybe* saw Cheryl but couldn't remember where."

Keelin softened when she realized how frustrated the man sounded. Perhaps he did have her best interests at heart by not wanting her along on the ransom drop. Only, she didn't happen to agree with his decision.

Leaning against the counter where she'd stacked the wine bottles the day before, Keelin said, "The apartment is across from a church."

"What?"

"The apartment where Cheryl is being kept."

"You know where my baby is?" Helen demanded.

"Not exactly. Not yet." Keelin looked at Tyler. "But now we can find it."

"What are we waiting for?" Taking the mug from her hand, Tyler set it down on the counter and turned her toward the front door.

"What about me?" Helen asked, getting to her feet. "I can't go dressed like this."

His expression cold, Tyler said, "*You* weren't invited."

"She's my daughter, too!" Helen screamed. "I may have been at fault when she got lost the first time, but she was in *your* custody when she ran away and got herself kidnapped. What kind of a parent does that make *you?*"

Helen's emotional outburst struck a responsive chord in Keelin, and she regretted suspecting her. No matter what mistakes the woman had made, she did seem to care about what happened to her daughter. Still, she didn't try to convince Tyler that they should take his ex-wife along. No more wanting to be in Helen's company than he did, she kept her peace as they started off.

They were well on the road before Tyler opened up the conversation. "We had it out this morning. I told Helen that when we found Cheryl, I planned on telling her that her mother is alive...*if* she doesn't already know."

"Then Helen won't be able to blackmail you any longer."

"No. She's off the gravy train. She'll have to take me back to court to get another penny out of me. I won't make things easy for her. Or for myself."

No wonder his ex-wife had appeared so truculent. Her source of income was gone, and Keelin had imagined all that concern was for Cheryl. More fool she.

"So tell me about the dream."

"I didn't dream last night," she said. "I woke up remembering the church steeple from the dream I had when we were returning from Wicker Park."

"What about other details?"

He didn't need the specifics about Cheryl's being tied and gagged, Keelin assured herself. "She was looking at the television, then out the window. That's all."

She wondered if he noticed the color stealing up her neck. Burning, she shifted and sank lower in her seat, grateful that he didn't pursue it. To her everlasting gratitude, he didn't say much the rest of the way to the Wicker Park area.

After crossing the six-corner intersection, he said, "I'll turn at the first side street and drive straight through unless one of us spots a church."

The first church they encountered stood across from old mansions and two-flat houses. Several more blocks of zigzagging the area, and they spotted a second church. Keelin looked to the other side of the street.

"A six-flat," she murmured. "And it has a stoop!"

Tyler immediately pulled the Jaguar into the only available parking spot on the block.

Keelin's pulse quickened as they approached the building. The church's steeple lay directly across from the third-floor apartments. Tyler held the outer door open for her. When she saw the chipped marble stairs in the vestibule, her excitement rose.

He quickly inspected the mailboxes and bells. "Look, no name on 3B."

"That must be it."

The inner door was ajar, so they walked right in and up the stairs. With each step, Keelin's heartbeat accelerated, and she sensed Tyler's tension increase. When they rounded the second landing, she put her hand on his arm. His jaw was set in a grim line, and yet somehow his glance told her so much more. Hope for Cheryl. Gratitude toward her.

As they reached the second landing, his hand shot out, indicating she should stay back. Keelin complied. She tried to breathe normally, but each intake of air was forced, and when Tyler knocked on the door to 3B, she forgot to breathe altogether.

No response.

Tyler knocked again, harder.

Nothing.

His third attempt shook the wooden panel in its frame, but still it roused no one.

"Damn!" His fist shot into the door. "We've got to find someone with a key."

Just then, the door across the way cracked open. Behind the chain, an elderly lady peeped out. Keelin recognized the woman even as she said, "Go away before I call the police!"

"I saw her before," Keelin whispered to Tyler. "I mean, Cheryl did when she tried getting away."

"I don't mean anyone harm," he assured the neighbor. "I'm just looking for my daughter."

"No one there. Left earlier."

"Maybe Cheryl is inside alone." Tyler raised his voice. "Cheryl, baby, are you in there?" he called, putting his ear to the panel.

Keelin strained but heard not the slightest sound. Disappointment filled her until Tyler tried the knob, and the door opened readily. He stepped inside the apartment. She followed directly behind him.

"You can't go in there!" the elderly neighbor called after them.

Keelin looked around, recognizing the shabby furniture in the unoccupied living room. The doors to the bedrooms and bath stood open. They were unoccupied, as well.

"Damn!" Tyler exploded. "They've moved her!"

"We were getting too close," she proposed. "Or perhaps Jack Weaver did last night."

Tyler didn't try to hide his disgust. "Let's get the hell out of here!"

She wanted to put her arms around him, but the stiff way he held himself was anything but an invitation. Comforting him could wait awhile. She followed him into the hall and noticed the elderly lady was still peering out at them. No doubt, she paid attention to anyone who came or went.

Keelin caught Tyler's arm to stop him from running off. "This man is looking for his child," she told the woman. "The people who rented that apartment are holding her against her will. We need to find them, but we don't know their names or what they look like."

The silver-haired head shook vigorously. "I can't help you."

"You must have seen something. Think hard," Keelin pleaded. "We're talking about a fourteen-year-old girl."

"Don't wanna get involved," the neighbor muttered, though she appeared torn.

"Please."

The woman looked them both up and down as if judging the veracity of their story before making up her mind. "Don't know any names. They were only there less than two weeks. In and out a lot. Never got a good look at *him,* though."

"But you did get a good look at someone," Tyler urged.

"The girl, once. And the woman. She didn't belong in this building."

"Why not?" Keelin asked.

"Her clothes. Too fancy."

"Can you describe her?"

"Pretty, with a good figure. Blonde. That's all I gotta say."

"Wait a minute," Tyler objected, but the woman closed the door in his face. "I could use the name and number of the management." When his raised request received no response, he said, "Come on."

"Should we ask someone else?"

"It's probably not necessary."

She didn't understand until they exited the building and he checked the side. High up, a plaque announced the building was managed by Damen Realty.

A moment later, they were on their way out of the neighborhood and heading for Tyler's office. He used the cellular car phone to call the authorities. He demanded they go over the apartment with a fine tooth comb and check out the identities of whoever had rented the place with the realty company, as well. Keelin could tell he didn't like the responses he was getting.

Dropping the cellular, he confirmed her suspicion. "They need a court order to get into the place and might need one for the realty."

"The authorities must abide by the law."

"If you ask me, the law is too slow."

"That they are. Why did you not give them the woman's description?"

"Maybe I should have given them her real name, as well," Tyler said caustically. "Except that, without absolute proof, I doubt the police would believe Vivian was mixed up with something as sordid as kidnapping."

Frustrated that they were stopped cold after such a promising start, Keelin wondered if Skelly might be of some help in getting the information on the kidnappers *his* way.

The Jaguar was soon crawling in the heavy traffic of Lincoln Park West.

"I can't wait for whatever the authorities come up with, Keelin. I'm going to spend my day seeing to the ransom money. My gut tells me I'm going to need it if I want her back."

"So you won't need me."

He glanced her way, his expression astonished. "That's not true. I do need you, Keelin. I told you so."

"Then take me with you when you deliver the ransom," she said stubbornly.

"But I won't put you in unnecessary danger. The last note was very specific about being alone if I didn't want anyone to get hurt."

She didn't continue to plague Tyler as she was tempted to do, merely waited until his vehicle was settled in the car park and they exited to the street.

"I shall leave you to your money gathering," she said.

Tyler already seemed distracted. "What about you?"

"I'll ring you later."

He squeezed her shoulders and brushed her temple with his lips. "I'll miss you."

She wouldn't let him soften her so easily. "You'll be too busy."

"Never too busy to think of you."

Never was an interminable amount of time. Knowing they didn't have that long to be together, Keelin wriggled free of his arm. "You have currency to collect, remember?"

She waited until he'd disappeared inside the L&O Realty offices before heading for the corner and the bus stop. She counted out exact change and slipped the coins into her pocket, then fished for two more quarters to buy a newspaper from a box. She was about to drop the money into the slot when she spotted Brock Olander on the street.

Furtively glancing over his shoulder as if afraid of being caught—by Tyler?—he then flagged down a taxi going south, and she caught a glint—a watch?—on his wrist.

He didn't see her.

Instinct and another convenient taxi waiting for the light to change convinced her to find out where Tyler's partner was headed. She raced across the street, waved over the yellow vehicle and hopped into the backseat.

"Follow that vehicle," she ordered her driver, a young Hispanic whose hair was shaved in lightning patterns around his head.

"Follow that cab." He pulled down his meter flag and gave her a gap-toothed grin.

"Pardon me?"

"In the flicks, they always say, 'follow that cab.'"

Amused despite the seriousness of the situation, she said, "Very well, then. Follow that cab."

Her vehicle lurched and shot forward. She sat back and kept an eye on Brock's taxi, now nearly a block ahead. Several cars had cut between them.

"You a spy or something?" the driver asked, skillfully maneuvering his taxi so that they'd passed two of those cars by the following intersection.

"No, of course not. Why would you think such a thing?"

"You got an accent. You're followin' someone." His eyes shifted from the traffic to the rearview mirror and looked at her. He smirked. "Ah, I get it. Boyfriend or husband trouble?"

"Both," Keelin impulsively lied. Her cheeks warmed.

"Don't worry. A pretty lady like you deserves a break," the driver said, gaining on another car.

Fortunately, Brock didn't go very far, and her driver stayed with him. A few blocks from her hotel, he alighted from his taxi and disappeared into an elegant old building. Her taxi slid to the curb, the driver keeping the vehicle a discreet distance back.

Handing him more money than the meter required, she said, "Wait for me," and slipped out of the backseat.

"I'll keep the motor running," the driver promised with another grin.

Keelin approached the building cautiously lest Brock spot her. But when she peered through the front door's glass insets, he was nowhere in sight. She entered the brass-trimmed wood-and-marble vestibule, thinking to look for a directory that might give her a clue as to whom he'd come to see. But the offices held only a single tenant.

Nathan Feldman Associates.

NATE FELDMAN SPRAWLED back in his leather chair, tempted to put his feet up on his marble desk and shout *Hallelujah!* But he held himself in check—wouldn't do to show how much this deal had meant to him—and lit a fresh cigar instead.

"Help yourself," he told Brock between puffs, indicating the fancy, hand-carved cigar box he'd picked up in Rio.

"Thanks."

Brock didn't look so well. His skin was pasty, and his hand trembled slightly as he took the cigar. He didn't even light it, just stared down at the rolled tobacco as if he didn't know what to do with it.

"Congratulations. I wasn't convinced you were up to the task. You even got the Uptown project. Good show!"

Brock's expression spelled guilt. "Tyler's had everything his way almost from the beginning."

Was that justification or regret he heard in the other man's voice? Nate wondered. Too late for him to back out now. Regret wouldn't fix things. Wouldn't bring that Smialek kid back to life, either.

"I expect you'll be out of L&O Realty first thing next week."

"So soon," Brock muttered, now sounding uncertain.

Nate figured he'd better boost the man's ego before he had a change of heart. "I understand a man has professional needs, Brock," he said heartily. "Our partnership will give you exactly what you deserve."

Brock nodded. "Your believing in me the way Tyler never did means a lot."

What a patsy! Nate thought. More to the point, their *temporary* partnership would give *him* the satisfaction of getting even, of gaining clients that Leighton would hate to lose. Hopefully, Smialek's lawsuit would drive the nail in Leighton's coffin, put him out of business completely and for good.

"Listen," Brock said, stuffing the cigar into the breast pocket of his jacket, "I'd better get back before Tyler suspects something."

"He's too preoccupied thinking about the kid."

"Still . . ."

Nate nodded. He lifted the briefcase and placed it on his desk. Then he slid a contract toward Brock. "Sign on the dotted line and it's all yours."

Hesitating only a moment, Brock signed and took the briefcase. "Here's to success."

Nate wouldn't argue with that. The moment the door closed behind the chump, he put his feet up on his desk.

"Hallelujah!"

Success in ruining Tyler Leighton had been his goal all along.

BROCK SET THE BRIEFCASE on Tyler's desk and opened it. Neat stacks of bills filled half the interior.

"A quarter of a million in cash like you asked for. Now, about that agreement . . ."

Tyler handed Brock a written guarantee that he would cooperate in dissolving the partnership. It also listed the assets that each would take with him, including the Uptown renovation that had been Tyler's baby.

"I wish you'd rethink things," Tyler said, even though he needed the money for Cheryl. "I meant it when I said we could work this partnership out. You could consider this money a loan."

Having done some soul-searching, he guessed Brock had been right to be dissatisfied. He only wished he'd come to his senses sooner, or that Brock had insisted on having a serious discussion about the situation—*before* things had come to a head.

"I've done enough thinking. I just want to get this over with." His face pasty, Brock skimmed the signed agreement and nodded. "I expect we'll get the ball rolling first thing next week."

Tyler couldn't believe it. He didn't even have his daughter back. What had happened to Brock? When had he become so hard-hearted?

"Next week," he promised.

Agreement in hand, Brock left, not looking nearly as happy as Tyler might have expected. Tyler wasted no time in opening his office safe and securing the briefcase. He would personally pick up the rest of the money the next day. He'd no sooner locked the safe when Alma buzzed him. Fearing that she would tell him that Helen was insisting on speaking to him *again*—she'd interrupted him twice so far—he was relieved to learn that Jack Weaver was in the reception area.

"Send him right in, Alma."

When the private investigator stepped through the door, he was wearing a satisfied smile. "I'm pretty sure I found the building where your daughter's being held."

Not having expected such luck, Tyler was nonplussed. "Where?"

"It's a six-flat building about a block off North Avenue," Weaver said, tempering Tyler's excitement. When the investigator gave the address, he was totally deflated.

"We already knew that, but she's been moved. The police have someone watching the place." Tyler checked his watch. "By now, they should have the court order to get inside and search. Not that I think it'll do any good."

"So the cops beat me to it. Sorry. But if I'd been on the case in the first place..." Looking chagrined, Weaver shrugged and turned to leave. "I'll send you my bill."

"Wait. What are you doing tomorrow?"

Stopped in the doorway, the investigator said, "Nothing I can't change."

"Good." Tyler wouldn't put Keelin in jeopardy, but Weaver was a professional. "Close the door a minute."

After ascertaining that the investigator had access to a handgun, he told Weaver what he had in mind.

KEELIN BARELY GAVE Jack Weaver a second glance as he left Tyler's office. Rather than waiting to be announced, she rushed right in and closed the door, bursting to tell him what she'd learned. To her frustration, Tyler was on the telephone.

"Hang up," she demanded, not trying to hide her urgency. "I must speak with you."

After a quick apology to the person on the other end, he dropped the receiver back into its cradle. "What's going on? Are you all right?"

"Has Brock been here yet?"

"A little while ago. He brought the money."

She took a deep breath. She'd known it! "Did he tell you where the money came from?"

"I didn't ask. Why?"

"I followed him."

"You what?" Tyler launched himself out of his seat.

"After you returned to the office earlier, he was on the street, looking over his shoulder... as if he didn't want to be seen... and he flagged a taxi. So I went with my instincts."

"And him. Where?"

"The Gold Coast." She lowered her voice. "Nathan Feldman Associates."

"You're saying he got the money from Feldman?"

"He entered the offices empty-handed and came out carrying a briefcase. Black leather."

With the vilest curse she'd heard pass his lips to date, Tyler yelled, "He's got some explaining to do!" and started to rush by her.

She practically threw herself in front of the door to stop him. "You cannot face him with this now."

"Why not? I'll break his damn neck!"

"If Vivian Claiborne was the woman in the apartment, chances are she was in on the scheme with Feldman. And if Brock is working with Feldman..."

He stared. "You don't think Brock *knew?* Christ, he could put Cheryl's life in jeopardy with a phone call!"

"Exactly."

He backed off and paced the length of his office. "Wait a minute. This doesn't make sense. If Feldman has my daughter, why would he give part of the ransom money to Brock to give to me? So he can get his own money back?"

"Think. What is it Feldman wants of you more than money?"

"My class," he joked, his voice bitter.

She didn't feel like laughing. "Perhaps you have a point."

"Afraid I can't give him that, not even in exchange for my daughter."

"But Brock is an extension of you."

Tyler's brow furrowed, then cleared. "And if Brock went over to Feldman, he'd be bringing half our clients with him. And the Uptown theater renovation that Feldman so desperately wanted. That, added to Smialek's lawsuit..." He fell silent for a moment, then said, "Looks like they've been conspiring to ruin me, doesn't it?"

"I'm afraid so."

He sank into a sofa, for the moment appearing utterly defeated. She quickly crossed the short space and tried to comfort him, even knowing that the only thing to salve his wounds was to have his daughter returned to him unharmed.

Believing with all her heart that she would not be seeing through Cheryl Leighton's eyes unless she had the means to save the girl, Keelin knew she would have to be present at the ransom drop, despite Tyler's objections.

But how to learn where the exchange was to take place?

STRUGGLING WITH THE KNOTS for what seemed like hours, she finally loosened the rope that bound her hands. Her heart soared with hope as she pulled them free, and the charms on her bracelet tinkled as if applauding. Next, she ripped the foul gag from her mouth, then worked on the rope binding her ankles.

In minutes, she was trying to stand, trying to see. Her head swam and her stomach lurched with all the trying.

The space was pitch-dark. Confusing. No, terrifying.

Which way? Which way?

Stumbling forward, hands out to catch the wall, she felt the faint pulse of the building under her palms, could swear she heard the thrum of its heartbeat. Blindly, she stepped wrong. The floor pitched beneath her feet, and when she went flying, the building rumbled with muffled laughter.

"Please!" she squeaked, her voice so dry it was nearly gone. "I promise I won't tell. Just let me out of here. I want to go home! I want my dad!"

But no one was around to hear.

Only the building.

And it wasn't going to let her go!

CHERYL LEIGHTON WOKE with a start, her heart hammering, almost certain she wasn't alone. She whispered, "Hello? Anyone there?"

Then she realized it felt more as though someone had been inside her nightmare with her than in this space. A feeling not altogether unfamiliar. She shuddered, and the skin along the back of her neck rose in bumps. Impossible. The dark was making her imagine things, making her lose her mind.

She never wanted to be in a dark space alone again.

Tears seeped from her eyes and threatened to choke her.

He'd moved her, brought her here that morning, had left her for most of the day. A building in the process of renovation. A big building. Familiar. Empty. No one to hear her scream, even though she wasn't gagged. But she heard plenty.

A couple in the alley getting it on.

A fight out front on the street.

The *tick-tack* of claws inside. *Rats?*

She trembled and worked at the ropes binding her hands. Her wrists were raw, her fingers sore. She paused, grasping one of her charms for comfort. Somewhere outside, an el train rumbled by. She had to get free. She had to get out.

But something told her she wouldn't succeed.

Because the building wouldn't let her go.

"TYLER?" Keelin stood in the center of his room, shaking so hard her teeth were clacking. "Are you awake?"

He mumbled an unintelligible answer, and she realized that he was in twilight land, halfway between awake and asleep. The full moon swept its beams through the open windows and across his bed. She saw him stir. The night sighed, and a breeze swept into the room, carrying the distinctive smell of the lake. She took comfort in her senses, in her freedom, in knowing she was not trapped like Cheryl.

Hesitating only a moment, she flew to the bed and climbed under the sheet, seeking Tyler's solidity for comfort. He'd wanted her here with him, but Helen had taken the room next to his, and Keelin had been uncomfortable accepting the invitation. So she'd insisted on sleeping in Cheryl's bed.

And had dreamed Cheryl's dream—rather, had been trapped in the girl's nightmare.

She shuddered, and as if he sensed something was amiss with her even in sleep, Tyler wrapped his arms around her and pulled her closer. Wide-awake, she huddled against the man she loved, knowing his daughter was terrified, knowing she couldn't tell him so. Tomorrow, he had to have his wits about him. Equally important, so did she.

Keelin let her eyes drift closed and listened to the steady beat of his heart. She could imagine herself falling asleep with him every night. If only their situation weren't so complicated. If only he weren't so opposed to lasting relationships. If only he loved her as she loved him. He'd said he trusted her, but enough to give her his heart?

His hand wandered along her waist and cupped her breast. Her tender flesh swelled against his palm, perhaps for the last time.

Swallowing hard, Keelin knew she would never sleep for thinking of it.

"Tyler," she whispered, giving him a gentle shake, "make love to me as if we might never have another chance."

"Mmm, is this a dream?" he murmured.

"A grand dream."

Suddenly, he was awake and awakening her body, murmuring her name softly, tenderly, kissing her, stroking her neck, suckling at her breast through the cotton of her gown. He slid a hand down to her hip, where his fingers gathered the material and edged it up with aching slowness. In return, she smoothed her hands along his naked chest and down the flat of his stomach, exploring all his hollows and curves as she had not been able to do before. Her fingers wrapped around him.

His hand slipped from the side of her thigh to the front. His fingers brushed her lightly, stroked her until she felt a damp flow. Her fingers stroked him until he was hot and heavy.

She joyfully opened to him.

She moaned as he stroked her delicate flesh, which was burning for deeper exploration. She drew him closer, then slid her leg up and around his thigh to provide him easier access. Resistance made him hesitate and lift his head from her mouth at last, but she couldn't wait any longer. Ignoring his questioning expression, clinging to his neck, she lifted her other leg and let her weight slide her where she wanted to be, one with him.

"Keelin . . ." he murmured in her hair. "Why . . . ?"

"Shh."

She rocked her hips to quiet any uncertainty, and Tyler responded, first with a shudder, then by moving with her. Waves of pleasure washed over her, and at last she knew what it was to feel complete. She grasped at his back, her nails digging into his flesh, silently urging him to do something, anything to help her find what lay just out of reach.

Like a man possessed, he drove into her, giving her more pleasure than she thought possible. And when she was certain there was no more to be had, his last thrust sent her spiraling out of her body to some other world.

Her cry was joined by his shout.

He collapsed on her. That he might crush her was of no consequence. She didn't want this moment to end, for she feared that once he released her, she would never know this feeling again. He was panting, his heated breath against her neck making her melt inside. She held him desperately, willing this moment to last forever.

Cradling her, Tyler eased his weight off her and took a big breath. His chest heaved, then quieted. She unwound her legs from his hips and sunk to the bed, her nightgown flowing over her thighs, the feeling as sensuous as the one inside her.

Tyler murmured, "The first time shouldn't have been like this."

She was stricken. "You're disappointed?"

"No, of course not." He captured her face in his hands and leaned his forehead against hers. "I mean it should have been better *for you.*"

"It could have been better?"

She couldn't imagine being the recipient of more pleasure than Tyler had already given her. He'd brought her to the stars and back. Even now, she was pulsing with the afterglow of their union. Unsure of what lay ahead for them, she treasured the lingering sensation.

His expression lightened. "I guess I meant *nicer.* Flowers. Champagne."

Relieved, Keelin smiled at his romantic concern. "I have no complaints."

"Nor do I," he said, brushing his lips gently across hers.

He held her quietly, his hand tracing her spine. For a few moments, she put aside all thoughts but the memory of their joining and the love she had for him. Her climax had been an afterthought, physically exciting and yet not as intense as the passions he aroused in her heart and soul.

Even as she drifted in the luxurious aftermath, snatches of Cheryl's nightmare pulled at her, uncertainty tearing at her momentary bliss. If things went wrong and his daughter was lost to him for good, Keelin knew Tyler would be destroyed. Now it was more than her own redemption for Gavin Daley's death that mattered to her.

What if, despite her determination, she failed the man she loved?

Chapter Eleven

Keelin awoke alone in Tyler's bed. Awake most of the night, she'd finally fallen asleep just before dawn, and now the morning had progressed without her.

She slipped back to Cheryl's room, where she hurriedly pulled on a dress and ran her fingers through her hair. Barefoot, she raced downstairs, and just in time.

She caught up with Tyler in the foyer—he appeared ready to leave.

"You're up." He sounded surprised but not displeased. "I left a note in the kitchen. Good. I'd rather say goodbye in person."

Goodbye?

The thought registered even as Tyler reached for her and drew her to him. She resisted. "Why were you going to leave without me?" she asked.

"You were sleeping so peacefully, I didn't have the heart to wake you."

When he brushed his lips over hers, she pulled her head away, unable to hide her disappointment. "Are you certain you aren't trying to be rid of me?"

Irritation crossed his features. "I've got a lot to do before—"

"And I can help."

"No. I want you out of this, now. I need to concentrate on Cheryl." His tone softened. "I don't want to have to worry about you, too."

He sounded as if he cared, she realized. But if he really cared, he wouldn't shut her out knowing what he did about her past mistake, about the guilt that had followed her for years. Or maybe he didn't really believe that she had it in her to set things right this time.

"You cannot do this without me," she said, as certain of this as she was of anything.

"I can and I will." He backed off, and a flash of regret washed over his face before he opened the front door. "And I hope you have the good sense to stay put until it's all over."

Good sense?

Keelin stood frozen to the spot until she heard the Jaguar pull out of the driveway. Then she ran to the door and threw it open in time to see the bottle green vehicle disappear.

"God bless," she whispered after him, hoping the goodbye was only temporary.

Taking a deep breath, she looked around. Helen's car was gone, as well. She was well and truly alone. She slammed the door and locked it.

Stewing over such heartless treatment, she put the kettle on and fetched some tea from her kit. The mixture of chamomile, vervain, peppermint, linden, lavender and lemon balm was a restorative meant to improve well-being and to lift the spirits. She could certainly use a good dose of spirit lifting so she could rationally decide what to do next.

By the time she'd had her tea and toast and had chosen not to feel sorry for herself, it was after eleven.

Bringing a mug of tea to Cheryl's room, she finished dressing and fixed her hair properly.

Then, as she sipped at the last of the brew, she found herself standing before Cheryl's shelves, pulling out the scrapbook with the photos of the girl and Tyler at the fair. Sitting cross-legged on the floor, she stared at the two of them. Even in this glossy still life, she could see how much they meant to each other.

She touched the girl's image, wishing she could see through Cheryl's eyes at will.

Thinking she might need to show someone a picture of Cheryl later, she looked for a shot of the girl alone. The last series in the album was of Cheryl's graduation. Keelin chose a five-by-seven blowup and carefully pulled the edges free from the stays that held the glossy in place on the page.

Something dropped from behind the print. Wondering what the girl had secreted, Keelin hesitated only a second before unfolding the note.

Tyler,
Our arrangement is no longer satisfactory. Call me to work out the details. 317-555-4362.

Helen

Keelin stared at the missive. Tyler's ex-wife.

Why hadn't he told her about the note? She had no doubts that Helen had been asking for more money. And Cheryl... how had the demand found its way to her... and what had the girl done about it? Cheryl must have guessed Helen was her mother or she wouldn't have hidden the note in her scrapbook.

Can't stay here any longer. Not one minute. No more lies.

Cheryl's thoughts came back to haunt her. Now they made sense. Had she contacted Helen? How to know? Keelin wondered. Cheryl didn't seem to keep anything in writing.

Unless . . .

Her gaze strayed to the computer. Skelly had given her a quick introduction to his computer when she'd been looking for those articles. She vaguely remembered his keeping his phone numbers and notes in different files, and Tyler had talked about Cheryl's navigating through cyberspace.

She approached the electronic beast. "Please God, that I may tame you," she whispered, drawing out a seat and finding the Power switch.

The computer energized, as did the monitor. Messages and colors flashed across the screen. Dread built in Keelin. What foolishness was this? She had no idea what she was doing. But when the computer settled, boxes that Skelly had called windows were on the screen, and in each box, small figures with names. She found one such figure labeled Notebook and clicked the mouse pointer on it.

She spent a frustrating fifteen minutes before managing to find the few file names and open the first on the list. She worked by trial and error. Nothing of value.

Terminal was equally unhelpful.

Cardfile was next. She was getting a handle on this process. Files were labeled Friend, Relative, Business and Other. She opened Relative and found a number for Tyler's mother in Florida and his sister in Kentucky. She tried Other. Only a single entry: Helen.

She recognized the telephone number as being the same as that in the note. Cheryl knew, then. Furthermore, she must have used the number, or why would she have entered it into her computer?

But Helen hadn't said anything about her daughter's contacting her...

Thoughtfully, she stared at the entry, wishing it could give her some answers. Then she carefully backtracked, closing the file, then the program, then the operations.

"Good beast," she said, patting the computer before shutting off the power.

Her next stop was the room Helen had used. Having no qualms about entering, she saw the unmade bed and the strewn towels on the bathroom floor. So Cheryl had inherited her mother's untidiness. But not one item that she could identify as belonging to Helen remained anywhere to be found. Not even a tube of toothpaste.

Helen was gone. For good, Keelin suspected.

That cinched it. She rang L&O Realty.

"Sorry, Miss McKenna," Pamela told her. "But Mr. Leighton stepped out."

Did his assistant sound nervous, or was it her imagination? Keelin wondered. "What time will Tyler return?" she asked.

"Uh, I'm not sure... but he said not to expect him until I see him." Pamela added, "He'll probably be in and out all day."

She wondered if Tyler's assistant knew why. More important, was Pamela aware of Brock's involvement with Nathan Feldman?

Every time she considered the situation, the resolution seemed more and more complicated, as if they were dealing with a large conspiracy of which Cheryl was only a small part.

Grand.

And she could not even speak to Tyler. He was out collecting the ransom. For all she knew, he could avoid her calls the entire day.

Frustrated beyond belief, she dialed Skelly's number at the station, but his taping was already in progress. She left a message for her cousin, asking that he ring her at her hotel later.

And then she searched Tyler's bedroom, hoping he'd been foolish enough to leave the ransom note for her to find. *Some* clue as to where he was to make the exchange.

No luck there or in his study, however.

After completing her search, she leaned back in Tyler's office chair and gazed at the framed photograph of Cheryl on his desk. So young to be hostage to some revenge scheme. Part of the girl's innocence and her faith in her fellow man would be shattered. Noting Tyler had set the charm they'd found at the band shell near his daughter's picture, she snatched it up. Staring at the perfectly crafted tiny fairy, she only wished the charm bracelet had the power to protect its owner....

About to replace the charm, she hesitated. She rolled the tiny bit of silver between her fingers and couldn't quite force herself to let it go. She slipped the charm into her pocket. Perhaps the fairy would bring *her* good luck. For the Fates seemed suddenly to have turned against her, she mourned.

Not that fate would stop her from being part of the night's dramatic events. If she had to, she would lie in wait for Tyler at L&O Realty. As Pamela had suggested, he would be in and out all day. Undoubtedly, he would be depositing each large amount of cash he collected in his safe. No doubt he would proceed to the exchange point directly from his offices.

And Keelin hoped to have the perfect opportunity to follow him.

"TOO BAD YOU CAN'T DREAM through the kid's eyes while you're awake," Skelly said after she'd explained her dilemma later that afternoon. "Then you could see where the bastards who are holding Cheryl take her."

Keelin was curled on the sofa in the sitting room of her suite, while her cousin paced, as if the outcome of the night's events were as important to him as they were to her.

"Being able to do so would simplify things. Too bad Gran never taught me how."

"Whoa!" He skidded to a halt. "You mean Moira indicated it's possible?"

"She spoke of having lucid visions," Keelin agreed, once again wishing she knew more about the process. Maybe then things would never have gotten to this point.

"But you've never tried it?"

"I regret not. I have no experience in the area of self-hypnosis."

"I got into self-hypnosis for a story." Sounding excited, Skelly perched on the sofa next to her. "That's how I quit smoking."

"Not quite the same task," she argued.

"No, but the principle's got to be similar. You relax, first your body—one part at a time—then your mind. You give yourself a suggestion to do whatever it is you want, but you package it in fancy wrappings."

She frowned at him. "I'm not certain that I understand."

"Like I had to think of something that would make me feel good if I wasn't smoking. Imagining a beautiful spot where I could swim for miles. Or climb mountains. Or run through fields. Things that took a lot of deep breathing. Things I couldn't do with tar-corroded lungs. See what I mean?"

"I . . . think so." Though the same methods might not help her unlock someone else's mind. "Perhaps we should keep to the original plan."

"Following Tyler?" Though he appeared a bit disappointed, he said, "Your call, cuz."

She gave Skelly a big hug. "I don't know how I'll ever be able to thank you properly."

"Hey, no big deal." While Skelly seemed somewhat embarrassed, he returned the hug and patted her on the back. "Hopefully, we'll get good news all around." To her questioning look, he said, "Dad's flying in tonight, remember."

Dear Lord, the reunion. She'd been so preoccupied that she'd forgotten the reason for coming to the United States in the first place.

"Aileen will meet him?" she asked.

"That's the plan."

"I hope your sister has as much influence with your father as you imagine."

Something had to go right, Keelin thought, trying to be positive. And surely Raymond McKenna couldn't be as stubborn as Tyler Leighton.

HER NERVES ON EDGE, Keelin gave a start when Tyler finally left L&O Realty, the loaded backpack in hand, shortly after 9:00 p.m. She grabbed Skelly's arm. "There he is."

Having lucked out, they'd been able to get a parking spot just down the street from the realty office more than an hour ago.

"Wait. He's not crossing to the car park," she said.

Skelly started the engine. "He's hailing a taxi."

Keelin didn't take her eyes off Tyler, who was barely a hundred yards away. She only wished she could see him better to judge his frame of mind. She only wished she were with him.

"Follow that cab," she said, grimacing.

As the taxi pulled away, so did they, only two vehicles in between. Keelin's sense of urgency pressed in on her, increasingly so as they continued in the same direction. Rather than turning west toward Wicker Park, as she'd suspected they'd be doing, the taxi was continuing south on Clark.

"Where could he be headed?"

"Your guess is as good as mine," Skelly said. "All kinds of places loaded with people between here and the Loop."

"I was imagining an area a bit more deserted," she admitted.

They'd gotten within blocks of her hotel before the problem of keeping up with Tyler began. Heedless of traffic, two couples raced across the street in the middle of the block. Skelly threw on his brakes. Several more vehicles inched in between them and Tyler's taxi, including a van.

"I can't even see him now," she complained as they came to an intersection where a group of burly young men crossed against the light. "Try to catch up, could you?"

But by the time the crossing was clear of pedestrians, the light had turned red.

"Damn!" Skelly's hand crashed into the steering wheel. "We've lost him."

Dismay filling her, Keelin said, "Perhaps you can find him again."

The light changed, and Skelly raced through the intersection and around several vehicles with the same expertise as had her taxi driver the day before. Ahead, she spotted several yellow cabs, any one of which could be Tyler's. The problem was compounded when two of the taxis turned off Clark, one in either direction. Skelly stayed with those that continued south, but when they drew closer, she could see a couple in each backseat.

"We really did lose him," she cried. "Now what?"

"Now it's time for you to develop a new skill," Skelly said, making a turn and racing down a darker side street. He pulled into the curb at a fire hydrant and cut the engine. "Think you can convince yourself to relax?"

Realizing what he expected of her, she opened her mouth to protest. But what choice did she have?

"Ready?" he asked.

She fumbled with her dress pocket. "I shall have to be."

"I'll talk you through it. Start by taking some deep breaths . . . in through your nose . . . out through your mouth. That's it, only slower."

Following Skelly's voice, she stared down at her palm. The ghostly illumination of a nearby streetlight allowed her to see Cheryl's fairy charm. She concentrated on it.

"Close your eyes ... let your body relax. Start with
your feet ... feel a little tingly sensation ... then your
ankles ... your calves."

Eyes closed, the charm pressed into her closed hand,
Keelin felt her body grow lighter and lighter as Skelly
helped her find the path she so desperately needed.

"You're drifting. Now clear your mind of all
thoughts but Cheryl. Concentrate on her ... on her
smiling face. She's happy, Keelin...."

For a moment, she envisioned a pretty young girl
with light brown hair being twirled around and
around. Cheryl threw her arms around Tyler's neck,
the motion setting the bracelet on her wrist to tinkling.

"I see her," she whispered. "With Tyler ... the fair
last summer."

"Good. You're on the right track. Look for Cheryl
wherever she is now," Skelly was saying. "She's
somewhere close by. Concentrate on her thoughts ...
her emotions ... what she's seeing...."

Her hand flexed around the charm, and in her
mind, she raced through the darkness.

*She stared out into blackness as her sore fingers
played over her bracelet for comfort. At least her
wrists weren't tied anymore. They didn't have to be.
She knew what would happen if she tried anything.
She'd seen the gun.*

"Dear God," Keelin whispered, the image dissolving instantly. "I believe they've threatened to shoot
her if she doesn't cooperate."

"You did it?" came Skelly's voice from somewhere beyond her new consciousness. "Don't let it go,
Keelin. Don't lose her. We can deal with the gun. Stay

with Cheryl. See through her eyes one last time. We've got to know where they're headed!''

Heart pounding, Keelin did as Skelly urged. Desperately, she clung to the charm in her hand and let her mind reenter the cosmos.

She was scared. More scared than she'd been in the apartment or the abandoned building. More scared than she'd been on the streets. She squeezed her eyes shut and bit her lip so she wouldn't cry like some baby.

Her dad was giving them lots of money for her, but what if he tried something brave to save her and they shot him anyway?

Then she'd have no one.

''Don't be scared, Cheryl,'' Keelin whispered. ''You're not alone, I promise. I won't let anything bad happen to you or your dad.''

Her heart skipped a beat, and her eyes flashed open as she thought she heard something weird...something inside her head.

Not the first time, either.

''We're almost there,'' came a voice from behind her, raised over the loud drone of the motor.

Their direction changed, and they hit some rough bumps. Cold water sprayed her. Shivering, she glanced over her shoulder, past the city's skyline, her eyes drawn to the bright, moving lights that were coming closer....

''What are you seeing, Keelin?'' came the voice outside her head.

''A Ferris wheel.'' The lit circle and spokes clear in her mind's eye, she said, ''They're drawing closer...coming in from the lake. I think...they *are* in a motorboat!''

"Keelin, let the image go for now. Let Cheryl go," Skelly urged, his voice excited. "You're back in the car with me. You can feel your body again. Your hands, feet and everything in between."

The unnatural darkness receded, and she blinked her eyes, felt the weight of the tiny charm in her palm. She uncurled her fingers and stared at it.

"I found her," she whispered, even as Skelly started the car. "I saw through her eyes...a giant Ferris wheel."

He nodded. "It's got to be the one at Navy Pier! You did good. And we're only a few minutes away."

They were the longest few minutes that she had ever experienced, even though Skelly drove like a madman, careering through the night, somehow managing to avoid several traffic-engulfed intersections for quieter ones.

Finally, the crowds couldn't be avoided, and their progress slowed. She glanced at the car clock—almost ten—and then straight ahead at a long pier swarming with people. Several tourist boats were docked along the pier.

The Ferris wheel seemed to grow larger as they approached.

"I believe we don't have much time," she told her cousin, her eyes glued to the lights.

"I'll let you off and park the car. Don't worry, I'll find you," he promised.

Keelin nodded and drew herself together. She was prepared for whatever was to come. This was it. Her chance to redeem herself. She only hoped that she could look forward to more. A future, for one. And, God willing, a future with Tyler. Heaven only knew what hand fate had dealt her, for uppermost in her mind was her solemn promise to Cheryl Leighton.

She would see that the girl and her father were both safe if it was the last thing she ever did.

THE BACKPACK SLUNG over his shoulder as casually as if he were carrying a change of clothing rather than a million dollars in cash, Tyler entered the Family Pavilion. Trying not to let his worry about Cheryl dull his senses, he dodged a passel of running kids while keeping out an eye for anyone too interested in his progress. If he were being watched, he couldn't tell. Finally, rounding a haphazardly parked baby stroller, he reached his objective—the escalator that would take him to the upper level Crystal Gardens.

Weaver should already be in the big, flashy building whose main feature was a miniforest of Arizona palm trees. Meant to be an oasis for winter fun-seekers, the space was a greenhouse, its transparent wall and ceiling panels supported by towering grids affording a view in every direction.

The moment he entered, Tyler searched the busy area for the private investigator. Black wrought-iron tables and chairs were mostly occupied, as were seats around the palm trees. But no Jack Weaver.

He checked his watch. Nearly ten. The fireworks display was set for ten-fifteen. Even now, couples and families were drifting to the outside upper-level deck to find a spot from which to watch.

Unsure of how things would go with the exchange, he wanted backup. Someone other than Keelin. He couldn't be put in a situation where his attention was split. He knew he'd hurt Keelin earlier by excluding her, but he would make it up to her. She had to for-

give him. He'd never known such a woman existed—
a woman who was a true innocent.

No one waited anymore, he thought, dazed by the
unspoken revelation he'd come to while making love
to her. At least not that long. Why had Keelin?

The answer was all too clear. Undoubtedly, she'd
been waiting for the right man. He could hardly believe it, but there it was. Keelin had waited to share
herself with someone special.

Special sure as hell didn't describe him.

He took a deep breath. His romantic desires would
have to wait. First things first. Cheryl.

Not liking firearms—especially not around so many
innocent people—he suspected Feldman or Brock or
whoever would deliver his daughter for the trade
would be armed. The private investigator's having a
handgun was supposed to be insurance, just in case
something went wrong. Tyler wasn't going home
without his daughter.

So where the hell was Weaver?

The knot in his gut loosened a moment later when
he saw the investigator stroll into the Crystal Gardens
through a southeast door. Wearing a glow-in-the-dark
plastic necklace and carrying a cotton candy like a
tourist, Weaver barely looked his way before finding
a seat. Relieved, Tyler strolled through the oasis toward the north end to wait as he'd been instructed.

He checked his watch. Ten o'clock.

The next fifteen minutes would be the longest of his
life.

Chapter Twelve

Keelin jogged a third of the length of Dock Street, pushing her way through gathering crowds, avoiding a couple on bicycles and several younger people on in-line skates. Farther down the south side of the pier, a mime was entertaining a group of teenagers, and a clown was twisting balloons into animal shapes for some small children. Families were swarming onto one of the tourist boats, while two other vessels were just pulling away from the docks. People were taking seats and watching the water as if expectant.

She knew they were gathering for the fireworks that the sign at the west entrance of Navy Pier announced in flashing lights. Aware of loud rock music from above, she stopped, breathless, and glanced up at what looked like a weird-shaped white parachute. It was, in fact, the roof of an open-air concert arena. She'd already passed beneath the lit Ferris wheel and merry-go-round. Hordes of people on the upper level gathered at the railing to stare out over the water.

She hadn't realized how big Navy Pier was. Cheryl could be anywhere.

What to do?

The Ferris wheel drew her.

Climbing over disgruntled visitors who were using the steps as seats, she reached the upper level, her gaze continually roaming the crowd. Hundreds of people in line for the Ferris wheel slowed her inspection and limited her line of sight.

How would she ever find Cheryl and her captors? An impossible situation, Keelin feared.

Unless...

Praying she could produce just one more lucid vision, that just one more time she could will herself to see through Cheryl Leighton's eyes, Keelin found a bit of unoccupied railing and pressed her back into the metal. Slipping a hand into her pocket, she grasped the fairy charm and closed her ears to the rock music and the raucous voices pummeling her. The constantly changing lights of the giant Ferris wheel that towered overhead mesmerized her.

She willed herself to relax. Legs...arms... body...mind. She breathed deeply, in through her nose, out through her mouth. She concentrated on the pattern of changing lights, envisioned the pretty face and long brown hair she'd only seen in photographs. Her eyes grew tired, her lids heavy. She let them flutter closed.

At first, her mind wandered through a dark space.

Then it raced faster and faster until she crashed into a million flickering lights.

Even with her eyes closed, she was still seeing the Ferris wheel, Keelin realized, though from a different angle....

CHERYL'S HEART POUNDED wildly as she was dragged along, bumped and jostled by tons of happy people. She glanced back past the Ferris wheel at the Skyline

Stage beyond. She'd been to a concert there once, with her friends. They'd all loved the place and had been looking forward to the next time.

After tonight, she never wanted to set foot on Navy Pier again.

For a moment, the Ferris wheel mesmerized her, and she got that sensation again, as though someone were inside her head, looking around. She must be going nuts.

Wanting to scream, she instead gasped, ''Who are you?''

''You know very well who I am.'' The grip on her wrist tightened. ''Stop dragging your feet.''

''I'm not,'' she answered sullenly as they passed the merry-go-round, and the now-familiar sensation receded as quickly as it had come.

She might have to do as she was told, but she didn't have to keep making things easy. All her fault. What a jerk! What a stupid jerk she was believing all those lies the woman had told her. How could she have trusted a stranger over her dad?

''Remember, there'll be a gun aimed at your father. You do exactly as you've been instructed if you want him to stay alive.''

Afraid she might screw up again, Cheryl wanted to cry. ''I trusted you. I wanted to be with you. Why did you have to turn out so awful?''

Through her tear-filled eyes, Cheryl thought the woman actually looked as if she might be sorry...but, as she was roughly shoved inside when she resisted going through the doorway leading into the garden, she figured that had to be her imagination, too.

TYLER'S NERVES WERE on edge from waiting for what felt like forever. He sat at the base of a palm tree, the backpack nonchalantly dropped at his feet. The Crystal Gardens had emptied out in anticipation of the coming fireworks. A glance at his watch told him it was nearly a quarter past ten. Only another few minutes, then.

He'd figured on their being exactly on schedule, and so he was looking directly at the girl who stood at the other end of the garden for several seconds before realizing he was staring at his own daughter.

"Cheryl!"

He bounded up and took a few steps toward her before caution intervened. Her eyes were wide, and she was visibly shaking, obviously scared and nearly in tears. His gaze flew over the few people who were not already outside for the fireworks. He recognized no one except his own private investigator, who was now on the alert.

"It's all right, Cheryl. Come to me, baby," Tyler urged, opening his arms, his heart in his throat.

He started toward her until her gaze shifted to somewhere over his shoulder. She pressed her fist into her mouth as if stopping herself from crying out. He slowed and glanced over his shoulder to see a fair-haired woman pick up the backpack.

But it wasn't Vivian who straightened and looked him straight in the eye.

"You should have called me like I wanted, Tyler," his ex-wife said. "If you would have been reasonable, adjusted our monetary arrangement like I asked, this wouldn't have happened."

Not having the slightest idea of what she was talking about, Tyler was stunned. Then his mind raced.

She hadn't done this alone. She'd had a male accomplice. Feldman or Brock?

"Take the money and run," he told her, turning back to his daughter.

But Jack Weaver was already jumping up from his table and grabbing Cheryl.

"Weaver, what the hell are you doing?" Tyler yelled as he started toward them.

The investigator whipped out the handgun he'd assured Tyler he owned. "I'd stay right there if I were you."

How stupid he'd been! He'd played right into their hands by believing Weaver really was Jeremy Bryant's replacement. He stopped, half the width of the garden still between him and his daughter. He felt sick inside.

"No, Jack, let her go!" Helen yelled from behind him. "Cheryl wasn't supposed to get hurt!"

"She won't if your ex-husband cooperates." Weaver glared at Tyler. "We're going to use your daughter as insurance that we get out of here alive and with the money."

From the corner of his eye, Tyler saw a bystander move toward the main pavilion door—to get help, he hoped.

"Jack, leave her be!"

"Helen, get out of here now with the backpack or I swear I'll shoot the kid!" Weaver threatened.

"I'm going." Helen's voice was shaky. "Don't hurt her, please."

Tyler heard her retreat even as his attention was distracted by a door opening behind the bastard. His heart lurched as a woman slipped through and slid back into the shadows.

Keelin!

"Leave Cheryl," he told the so-called private investigator. "All I want is my daughter. I promise I won't come after you." Though he'd use all his clout to get the authorities to do so later.

"No deal, Leighton. I don't believe you."

Tyler felt impotent as Weaver backed up toward the door, Cheryl in tow. This couldn't be happening! But what could he do without endangering his daughter's very life?

Suddenly, Keelin closed the gap between herself and them. Before a frantic Tyler could think of a way to stop her from doing anything foolish, a burst of sound reverberated through the building, an explosion of red-and-blue light reflected in the transparent panels all around them.

The fireworks seemed to fill the hall, effectively distracting Weaver. His gun swung out as he turned toward the source of the threat, and Keelin lunged forward, grabbing his wrist.

"Get away, Cheryl!" she screamed. "Now!"

Tyler was already running as Cheryl screeched and struggled and somehow loosened Weaver's grip on her. Then she was flying toward him blindly, tears pouring from her eyes, her flight backlighted by a series of green flashes that built one upon the other.

"Dad, oh, Dad, I'm sorry."

Throwing his arms around his daughter, he hugged her tight. He was speechless with gratitude. But his thankfulness was tempered by the scenario before him. Weaver freed his hand and struck out, clipping Keelin in the chin with the gun's muzzle. Dazed from the hit, she tottered, and the bastard took the advantage, replacing one hostage for another. Before Tyler could free himself from his daughter's tight grip, Weaver had hooked his arm around Keelin's neck.

"Stay right where you are, Leighton, or she dies." The gun was snugged in the halo of her hair.

"Let her go when you get outside." Tyler's order was backed by the blasts of a series of rockets that trailed white against the dark sky.

"I'll let her go when I'm damn well ready!"

"I shall be fine, Tyler," Keelin assured him, though she didn't sound convincing. "See to your daughter."

Weaver changed direction, heading for a north door. Keelin stumbled and was jerked hard for her clumsiness.

Tyler sweated and tightened his grip on his daughter. If anything happened to the woman he loved, it would be on his conscience. He'd trusted the wrong person to help him. He'd excluded Keelin. No. The problem was including her in the first place. If he hadn't, this wouldn't be happening now. Self-deprecating thoughts raced through his mind as fast as the fireworks burst in the sky.

He should have known Keelin would find a way to put herself in the middle of things. But how to get her out? He didn't trust Weaver to allow her to live when he was done with her. But how could he go after her without leaving Cheryl alone?

Before he could think of what to do, yet another person burst into the garden, as the sound of whining rockets pierced the air.

Wild-eyed, the disheveled man took in the scene. "Leighton, where's Keelin?"

Tyler took a breath of relief. "You must be Skelly."

"Forget the introductions. Where is she?"

"In big trouble. Stay with my daughter while I go after her."

Cheryl clung to him. "Dad, don't leave me!"

"You'll be safe with Skelly," he assured her, pushing her toward the other man. "Keelin trusts him, and that's good enough for me."

He started off.

"But, Dad, wait!" Cheryl wailed.

Tearing another hole in Tyler's heart. He stopped and faced his daughter. "I can't let anything happen to the woman I love any more than I could to you," he said, praying she would understand.

Cheryl hesitated only a second. She sniffed and dashed a tear from her cheek. "They have a boat. It's tied up on the north side of the pier. Hurry before they hurt her!"

Like they'd hurt Cheryl? he thought grimly.

Wondering that a fourteen-year-old could be worried about someone else after what she'd been through, he ran out to the open upper deck under a canopy of blurred color, half-blind from the emotions affecting his vision.

"SHE'S THE ONE, isn't she, Skelly?" Cheryl asked, wiping away her tears as her father disappeared.

She didn't like his going after her mother and her awful boyfriend, but the woman who'd helped her didn't deserve to be hurt, either. Somehow, she just knew her dad would make everything all right.

"Keelin's the one what?" Skelly shouted above another series of explosions.

Embarrassed, she couldn't quite meet the handsome man's eyes. "Um, you wouldn't understand."

Skelly lifted her chin. "Women usually find it pretty easy to talk to me."

Cheryl bit her lip. "She was . . . at least I . . . you'll think I'm crazy."

"Try me."

"I swear someone was inside my head." The words spilled out so fast they were nearly one. *"Her."*

Skelly smiled. "My cousin Keelin is an unusual woman. You're not crazy," he assured her as four uniformed police burst into the garden from the main hall.

"Hands up and get away from the kid," one of them yelled.

Skelly immediately complied. "I'm afraid we have a lot of explaining to do," he told her. In a lower voice, he added, "Uh, I'd suggest we keep what you just told me between us, though."

"Right. *They'd* think I was nuts for sure." Though she'd never been so happy to see cops in her entire life.

"Are you all right?" a fatherly type asked her.

Cheryl nodded. "He's okay," she said, referring to Skelly, who still had his hands raised. "But his cousin and my dad—" she nearly choked "—they could be hurt bad. Help them, please. The people who were holding me are real dangerous." She couldn't call Helen Dunn her mother. "Their boat is tied up on the north side of the pier."

"Giordano, stay with these two and get the whole story," the fatherly type said. He motioned the other two cops to follow him and raced for a door.

Giordano was a pretty, dark-haired woman with sympathetic brown eyes. "If the kid thinks you're okay, you can lower your hands," she told Skelly. She pulled out a notebook and indicated they should both sit. "Now, about that story."

Cheryl began with her finding the note and deciding to meet the mother she'd been told was dead.

KEELIN TRIED TO KEEP her head, but under the circumstances, it wasn't easy. His gun pressed into her side, his other arm around her as if they were lovers—no doubt, in case anyone noticed them—Weaver had hauled her around the back end of the stalled Ferris wheel. Nothing was moving during the fireworks display. And since everyone's attention was glued to the south lakefront, no one paid them any mind when he forced her down the ramp toward the dock level.

"Did Jeremy Bryant put you up to this?" she asked, pushing the question past the lump in her throat.

"The geezer doesn't have a clue. Cheryl's grieving mother sent Bryant on a wild-goose chase to Indianapolis to get him out of the way."

The sky lit with a myriad of trembling colors, and Weaver popped her inside the dock-level building, this time to cross through the car park. The explosives rang hollowly through the poorly lit, dank garage. Keelin thought fast, wanting to get as much information as possible out of the man. Helen's taking Cheryl at the same time Feldman was trying to ruin Tyler was too convenient to be mere coincidence.

"Were you working with Nate Feldman all along?" she asked as they dodged a couple of cars parked too close together and hurried through an empty slot.

Weaver seemed surprised at her acuity. "Feldman sent me to find Leighton's ex."

Eureka! Gathering her courage—she would rather think of anything but the gun he held—she doggedly kept on in the belief that Weaver would want someone to realize how clever he'd been.

"How could Feldman know Helen Dunn was alive?"

"That blond broad he's been showing around—she found Helen's demand for more money to keep playing dead. It didn't take much to seduce Leighton's ex," he bragged. "Not that I'm complaining. Didn't take much to get Helen to spill her guts about her ex and what he owed her. Took even less to convince her that if we snatched the brat, Leighton would pay anything to get the kid back."

So Vivian had had only a minor role in the drama, and Helen had been duped, probably didn't even know anything beyond her own involvement.

As Weaver shoved her through a door to the north side of the pier, she asked, "How did you hook up with Nate Feldman in the first place?"

"Did some work for him on one of Leighton's buildings in Wicker Park. Feldman didn't want it to meet city inspection."

Horrified, she said, "But that's the building where the Smialek boy died!"

"Shame about the kid." Not that he sounded sorry. "Shame you put it together, too."

Keelin recognized a threat when she heard one. Though the gun was still pressed into her side as they approached the boat where Helen already waited, the idea of her dying somehow seemed surreal.

"You're the one who attacked me in the park, aren't you?"

"And you owe me a Rolex."

While a series of fireworks rent the sky above the pier's buildings, she calmly asked, "Do you plan on shooting me?"

"Won't have to," Weaver said with a brutish laugh. He pushed her forward so that she went flying down into the boat. "I can take this baby far enough out that you'll never be able to swim back."

Keelin heard his last words through a daze of pain. Crumpled on the floor where she'd landed between the middle and back seats, she saw him jump down after her.

"What are you talking about, Jack?" Helen asked nervously. "We only planned to get Tyler's money, not kill anyone."

"Plans change," Weaver said grimly, cranking the engine to life. "Here, hold this on her. You let her go and it's your neck."

"Jack, please..."

Still stunned, Keelin pushed herself into a sitting position and noted that while the gun was pointed her way, Helen seemed distracted, truly upset. Her hands were shaking. Perhaps Keelin could capitalize on that.

"He's using you, Helen," she said as Weaver leapt up to the dock and began untying one of the lines. "He was paid to find you."

"Shut your mouth, bitch!"

Wide-eyed, her face cast a sickly green by the mercury-vapor lights, Helen said, "That's not true, is it, Jack?"

"Of course not, baby. She'd say anything to turn you against me."

This repulsive man was so arrogant that when he lied he didn't even look at the woman he'd duped, Keelin realized. Nor did he notice the movement in the shadows mere feet from where he stood, his attention focused on untying the last line.

Emboldened with sudden hope, she pulled herself to her feet and pressed Helen. "A crooked businessman named Nate Feldman put Weaver up to finding you and seducing you to get at Tyler."

"I said shut your damn mouth!" Weaver spun around, his attention now directed at her. "Or maybe I won't wait to let the fish get you."

Another burst of twinkling blue-and-white lights revealed a figure running toward them even as Weaver hurled himself into the craft and took the wheel. She nearly fainted with relief when she realized Tyler had come to her rescue. The explosion of accompanying sounds covered his footsteps as the craft slowly turned, its prow headed toward the middle of the lake.

Then Tyler leapt.

"Jack!" Helen screamed too late.

Keelin's heart was in her throat as Tyler flew through the air. His foot touched the side of the boat; his momentum kept him airborne. Even as Weaver turned, Tyler was on him, the thud on contact audible.

The men went down in a heap, Tyler on top. But Weaver was younger and undoubtedly stronger, considering his massive physique. Keelin held her breath as they rolled in the confined space, their arms flashing, the sounds of their fists contacting flesh more imagined than heard beneath the increasing cacophony of the fireworks display. Rockets were bursting in the sky as fast and furiously as the men were hitting each other.

Suddenly, Tyler flew back, his arms flailing, and Weaver was instantly on his feet and after him. Forgetting Helen for a moment, Keelin looked around wildly for something loose that she could use as a weapon. Her gait was unsteady as the boat slowly continued moving out into the lake.

She was wondering if a loose flotation cushion could do any damage when Helen ordered, "Just stay put." Her lover was still pounding her ex-husband with his fists.

"Is that what you want?" Keelin asked, revolted by the brutality. "You want to see Tyler dead because he divorced you?"

"He stole my child from me!"

"He *paid you* to stay out of your child's life because he wanted to protect her. And you readily took his money."

The gun wasn't even pointed at her anymore, Keelin realized. Helen's heart wasn't in this. Cheryl's mother might be greedy, but she obviously wasn't given to violence. This time, she'd chosen the wrong man to partner.

"Weaver's been working for Feldman for a while," Keelin yelled to be heard. The fireworks display was coming to a dramatic climax, layers of color building on one another. "He made a few adjustments in one of Tyler's buildings that was being renovated. The result was a child's death."

"You're lying!"

"He would have killed Cheryl if he'd had to!"

Helen's mouth gaped, but she couldn't seem to force out a denial.

"Perhaps he'll kill *you* for the money."

Suddenly, Weaver cried out. Keelin saw his head snap back and his body jerk. Tyler took the advantage, grabbing the man by his shirtfront and heaving him into the windshield. A panicked Weaver scrambled over the glass and onto the hood of the prow. Tyler vaulted onto a seat and followed.

Keelin held her breath as the men tightly circled one another around the confined space. Tyler found an opening and clipped Weaver's jaw, stunning and then pummeling him until the younger man collapsed over the bobbing prow.

Appearing ready to pass out himself, Tyler stumbled toward them.

"Are you all right?" she yelled worriedly, rushing between the seats to him.

Tyler leaned forward, his hands against the windshield, gasping for breath. "I'll survive."

She reached up and touched his bruised and bloody face. "Foolish, foolish man."

"I wasn't about to chance living without the woman I love," he said, the unexpected declaration thrilling her.

"She may have to live without *you!*" came a raspy voice from behind him.

Under a canopy of colored brilliance combined with smoke that shadowed the sky as far as the eye could see, the scenario played out in slow motion before Keelin's horrified eyes.

Weaver was on his feet, his hand raised and grasping something gleaming and sharp. His energy spent, Tyler obviously had to force himself to turn around to face the aggressor once more. He exposed his chest even as the man's arm began its downward arc.

Suddenly, Weaver jerked and froze, a surprised grimace distorting his features. His chest bloomed dark against his lighter shirt. His fist opened and the weapon fell, clattering and slipping into the lake. Like a felled tree, Weaver followed.

Keelin didn't even hear the splash. Then her gaze flew to a dazed Helen, still pointing the gun straight where her lover had stood.

"OUR FINAL REPORT IS an update on the disappearance and recovery of North Bluff teenager Cheryl Leighton," Skelly told his television audience. "A fantastic story of greed and violence. A complex and far-reaching plot was allegedly hatched by businessman Nate Feldman, seen here as police arrested him early Sunday morning."

Snugged in the crook of Tyler's arm at his home, Keelin watched "The Whole Story" with him, nervous about his reaction to her cousin's coverage. Skelly focused on Feldman himself, leaving out the exact details of Tyler's twelve-year monetary arrangement with Helen, as well as Keelin's own paranormal connection with Cheryl. His discretion surprised and pleased her, though she knew at least some of the details were bound to come out during Feldman's trial. Helen had already pleaded guilty to kidnapping and extortion, but also pleaded self-defense in her lover's death—Lake Michigan's waters still cradled Weaver's body.

As far as anyone knew, Vivian and Brock had only been involved peripherally, and while in love with Brock, Pamela had remained professionally loyal both to Tyler and L&O Realty, so Skelly never even made reference to them.

"In a bizarre twist," Skelly went on, "Feldman is also allegedly responsible for the unsecured porch railing that caused the death of Harry Smialek, the

Wicker Park boy who died on an L&O Realty renovation site. . . .''

Tyler had already received apologies from the Smialeks and had learned that their lawsuit against L&O Realty had been instigated by one of Feldman's lawyers.

To Keelin's relief, Cheryl was more resilient than she imagined. The girl hadn't invaded her dreams at all since the rescue. And even now, Cheryl insisted on being with her friends since everything was back to "normal." Keelin knew Tyler had made an appointment to take Cheryl to a family therapist, but instinct told her the teenager would fully recover.

"At least this story has a happy ending," Skelly was saying, the visual a shot of Cheryl wrapped in a battered Tyler's arms.

And for her, a new beginning, Keelin thought, free at last of the guilt that had haunted her. She had finally put the ghost of Gavin Daley to rest.

Skelly was on camera once more. "Tomorrow, a story on Lily Lang, 'the Blond Temptress,' who, convicted of murder, escaped from prison thirty years ago this week."

Tyler pointed the remote at the television and turned it off. "Maybe your cousin's not quite the sleazoid I accused him of being."

Equally pleased, Keelin agreed, "I think there's hope for Skelly yet." He'd even asked for their blessing before doing the follow-up.

"What about us? Is there hope for us?" Tyler asked, the question making her heart leap.

Though they'd professed their love for each other after their night of terror had ended, the past two days had been divided up between the police and sleep,

Cheryl's well-being and Keelin's family matters. While Uncle Raymond had greeted his long-lost niece with enthusiasm, Aileen had suggested she wait a bit before broaching the subject of the reunion.

And amid all the chaos, she and Tyler had not gotten around to discussing *them*.

"We do come from different worlds," she reminded him.

"But not different planets. I'm sure you've heard of jet travel."

She frowned. "You would be happy with a long-distance relationship?"

"Certainly not." He kissed her nose and tightened his grip on her. "The closer the better. I meant we could be an international family with two homes if that would make you happy."

Her pulse raced and familiar yearnings filled her, yet she argued, "I have a business, a herbalist shop. I have a responsibility to my two partners."

"We'll make arrangements for someone to represent you...or you could sell your share. If you wanted to."

"Either is a possibility," she said. "But there are more personal differences."

His eyebrows shot up. "You mean because you're a woman and I'm a man? I believe that's the way it's supposed to be."

Not smiling at his attempted humor, she said, "I come from a Catholic country."

He immediately grew serious. "I'm open-minded and flexible. Isn't it possible to work something out?"

Before meeting Tyler, she had never considered she might fall in love with someone from another country, much less someone from another faith. Her Aunt

Rose had faced the same dilemma, and her determination to marry the man she loved had caused the initial rift between the McKenna triplets. But Keelin understood exactly how her aunt felt, for she was of the same mind. Tyler was a good man. For herself, she could find none better.

"Two people who love each other can always find a solution," she said solemnly.

"Like marriage?"

She softened in his arms. "Are you asking me to marry you, Tyler Leighton?"

"I am, Keelin McKenna. Cheryl has already given her approval."

Her heart soared, and the differences were forgotten. "Then we must hurry. Make plans immediately—"

"Whoa." He laughed. "I believe the red tape might take more than a few days. And what about your family? Don't you want to give your parents and siblings enough time to get here?"

Suddenly dreading what Da would have to say on the subject, not wanting to spoil the moment by discussing his possible wrath, she murmured, "'Tis nearly a month after my thirty-third birthday now. I cannot wait for long if I am to accept my grandmother's legacy."

"And what legacy would that be? If it's money you're worried about—"

"Money is the last thing Moira McKenna would have worried over for her nine grandchildren." She quoted, "'I leave you my love and more. Within thirty-three days after your thirty-third birthday— enough time to know what you are about—you will have in your grasp a legacy of which your dreams are made. Dreams are not always tangible things, but more often are born in the heart. Act selflessly in another's behalf, and my legacy shall be yours.' "

"A lovely thought."

"Moira was a lovely woman."

"And has an even lovelier granddaughter."

With that, Tyler kissed her so lovingly that Keelin realized that the dreams born in her own heart had already come true.

HARLEQUIN®

INTRIGUE®

COMING NEXT MONTH

#385 BULLETPROOF HEART by Sheryl Lynn
Lawman

Reb Tremaine appeared on the Double Bar R, his sexy lips saying he could handle horses and his eyes saying maybe he could love a widow like Emily Farraday. But Emily was in trouble. And the danger didn't stop when she realized that everything Reb had told her about himself was lies....

#386 TELL ME NO LIES by Patricia Rosemoor
The McKenna Legacy

Rosalind Van Straatan needed to know the truth about the night her legendary grandmother confessed to a murder she probably didn't commit. The irreverent and disturbingly sexy Skelly McKenna wasn't exactly her first choice of investigative partners; unfortunately, he was her only choice.

#387 SPENCER'S SHADOW by Laura Gordon
The Spencer Brothers

Anne Osborne desperately needed a hero, but Cole Spencer didn't agree with his brother that he was the best man for the job. But then he gazed into Anne's trusting eyes, and he knew he'd go to the ends of the earth to protect this classy lady from a ruthless killer who thought Anne knew too much.

#388 A BABY'S CRY by Amanda Stevens

Ten years after Dillon Reeves walked out on her, Taylor Robinson had reason to believe that their child was not stillborn, as she'd been told. Dillon had never known about the pregnancy, but would he agree to help Taylor find their child?

AVAILABLE THIS MONTH:

#381 RULE BREAKER
Cassie Miles

#382 SEE ME IN YOUR DREAMS
Patricia Rosemoor

#383 EDEN'S BABY
Adrianne Lee

#384 MAN OF THE MIDNIGHT SUN
Jean Barrett

Look for us on-line at: http://www.romance.net

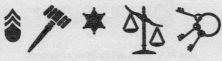

REBECCA

43 LIGHT STREET

YORK

FACE TO FACE

*Bestselling author Rebecca York returns to "43 Light Street"
for an original story of past secrets, deadly deceptions—and
the most intimate betrayal.*

She woke in a hospital—with amnesia...and with child.
According to her rescuer, whose striking face is the last
image she remembers, she's Justine Hollingsworth. But
nothing about her life seems to fit, except for the baby
inside her and Mike Lancer's arms around her. Consumed
by forbidden passion and racked by nameless fear, she
must discover if she is Justine...or the victim of some mind
game. Her life—and her unborn child's—depends on it....

Don't miss *Face To Face*—Available in October, wherever
Harlequin books are sold.

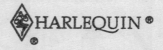

HARLEQUIN ®

43FTF